Murder on Time

ALSO BY ROGER SILVERWOOD

MURDER On TIME

ROGER SILVERWOOD

JOFFE BOOKS

Revised edition 2025
Joffe Books, London
www.joffebooks.com

First published in Great Britain in 2021

This paperback edition was first published
in Great Britain in 2025

Cover art by Nick Castle

ISBN: 978-1-80573-205-1

ONE

A1, Lincolnshire
Friday, 8 November, 11.30 p.m.

The chauffeur-driven Rolls-Royce pressed northwards along the A1, ferrying Miles Persimmon, film producer and director, and his wife, actress Lisa Maria Gooden, from the London Film Awards ceremony to their country home on the outskirts of Bromersley.

The inside lights of the Rolls turned off, they were both dozing on the lowered back seats of the limousine, made cosier with cushions and car rugs.

A few strands of greying hair fell over one of Miles Persimmon's eyes. His black tie and collar button were undone. From time to time he pulled a silver flask from his pocket and took a sip from it.

Lisa always looked beautiful. Even after an hour or so dozing in the limousine she still looked as delightful as she did on the big screen and on the stage accepting awards.

The limousine suddenly braked, swerved and then continued as before.

Lisa opened her eyes. 'What's happening?'

Miles wrinkled his nose in displeasure. 'Go back to sleep,' he said, taking the opportunity for a sip of brandy from his pocket flask.

Lisa glared at him. 'I hope you're not going to be on the bottle again this weekend.'

'I'll do as I please,' Miles said. 'Go back to sleep.'

'You're always so objectionable when you're tanked up.'

'You're objectionable *all* the time,' he said, with eyes closed. 'My drinking helps me to tolerate you.'

She looked at him for a few seconds and pulled a sour face. 'You've changed.'

'Do you know something?'

She waited. Said nothing. She knew he would continue with some insult.

'The more I drink, the more I am aware that you being objectionable is inconsequential. You won't be here much longer to annoy me. You're always griping about what I do. I don't spend a tenth on booze what you spend on jewellery.'

Lisa put her hand up to her cleavage and felt a large pear-shaped diamond suspended on a platinum chain. 'I'm very fond of my jewels, I must say. I get a lot of pleasure out of them. And they're an investment for my old age, which I hope to enjoy, while you are heading for dialysis, a wheelchair and an early death.'

Miles energetically rearranged his pillows and thumped them. 'And you're heading for . . . for something to shut your mouth. I am tired out and I have a lot on my mind. This new film . . .'

'Have you got a leading man yet?'

'No. I haven't even got a leading woman.'

Lisa's eyes flashed. She propped up on one elbow. 'I'm your wife. I took it for granted it was mine. Elaine Zimmerman said she wrote it with me in mind.'

He closed his eyes, yawned and then muttered, 'You're too old.'

Her mouth opened wide and her eyes stuck out like cherries on their stalks. 'Too old! I can play *any* age and you know it. I suppose you'll end up giving it to Mimi Montgomery,' she said. 'For a part like that, she'd drop them for anybody.'

'*She's* too young,' Miles said angrily. 'And there was a time, *Miss Lisa Potts*, when I dragged you out of the gutter, washed you, fed you, dressed you and taught you how to act. And *you* didn't even wear any to drop.'

'And you couldn't leave me alone,' she said. 'You were insatiable. Even in a changing cubicle in that gown shop on Knightsbridge. Huh! Well, I might just as well wear a suit of armour for what use you are to me now.'

Miles sat up. He was suddenly wide awake. He raised the back of his seat to the vertical position and brushed the strands of hair away from his face. 'After pointing out the fact that our marital relationship is over, it simplifies what has been on my mind for some months. Very soon, I have to go to Ireland with some execs on a search for exteriors for my next film. Then, Lisa, in the following few weeks, I am going to murder you.'

Lisa's heart missed a beat.

'Don't be so ridiculous,' she said.

Her mind raced. Her stomach felt empty. She shivered, tucking the car rug round her feet. She knew Miles could do it. And get away with it. She must say something.

'We could get a divorce,' she said. 'We could divide the farm into two. Or we could simply separate.'

'No,' he said. 'That means you would still be around annoying me. No, I have given it a lot of thought. I have had enough of you. There is no other way. I have to murder you.'

* * *

Bromersley, South Yorkshire
Saturday, 9 November, 11 a.m.

A man was sitting alone at a piano. A lit cigarette dangled from the corner of his mouth.

He was in a darkened room. The only light was from a lamp on the music stand illuminating the keyboard, which had an overfull ashtray resting precariously on the keys.

The man played three notes in quick succession, then he played them again slowly. Then he added more notes to play three full chords. Then he changed one of the notes and repeated the routine.

As he was tapping away, the door opened, letting daylight briefly into the room. A burly man pushed a smaller man, who was wearing a blindfold and had his wrists roped together behind his back, into the darkened room and closed the door.

The big man said, 'I've got Piggott, boss.'

After a few moments, without looking up, the man at the piano stopped tapping the keyboard. 'About time.'

Then he turned to the blindfolded man. 'Are you Cecil Piggott, the scrap metal man?'

'Yes. Who are you? Where am I? What is this?'

'Shut up and listen. Are you the father of Arthur Piggott?'

'Yes, but I can't talk to you like this. Who are you? Take this blindfold off.'

'*No!*'

'This is bloody outrageous! Where *am* I?'

'What does it matter where you are? Don't keep babbling on. Your time is running out, friend. Where is your son, Arthur?'

'I don't know. He comes and goes. He does as he likes. What do you want with him?'

'I can't find him. And it simply won't do. No, it will *not* do. It is putting my book-keeping into unnecessary disorder.'

Cecil Piggott had no idea what this man was talking about. He waited. Surely an explanation would be forthcoming. He must give nothing away.

The man at the piano continued, 'As an ever-loving father it surprises me that you don't know where your boy is.'

'He's twenty-six. Like I said, he does as he likes.'

'Well, Cecil . . . I can call you Cecil, can't I? It's like this. If he don't present himself to me in his best suit, with a smile on his face and a pocket full of folding stuff in the near future, I fear he will suffer a sudden shortness of breath.'

Piggott's jaw dropped. 'You . . . you can't mean you would *kill* him?'

'Oh you're very quick, Cecil. You catch on real fast. I'm beginning to like you, Cecil. We've got a lot in common.'

'But, I don't understand . . .'

'He didn't play the game, friend. He's got to play the game.'

'What game? What are you talking about?'

'He's got to play the game . . . according to the rules.'

'What rules?'

'The rules of life.'

'I don't know what you mean.'

'Look, Cecil, I'm a reasonable man. A *very* reasonable man. Anyone that knows me will tell you that. I am well known for my decency and fairness.'

He broke off and looked directly at the heavy. 'Well, Mr Crum, isn't that so?'

The heavy looked back at him. 'What's that, boss?'

The man at the piano glared back at him. *'Aren't I well known for my decency and fairness?'* he said icily.

'Oh yes, boss,' Crum replied mechanically with a knowing smile.

He continued, 'It's like this. If you do a favour for somebody, he owes you one. That's fair enough, isn't it? Well, I did a favour for him, therefore *he* owes *me* one. That's quid pro quo isn't it?'

'I suppose so,' Cecil Piggott said.

'So time rolls by, and eventually the time comes when I call in that favour. He understands that, but he don't want to know about it. He don't want to pay, you see. He runs away from the job, and to make it worse, he calls in the fuzz. Yeah. He calls in the fuzz for *his* protection. Now that's not nice and it don't do my blood pressure any good at all. Being smart, I keep myself out of both the fire *and* the frying pan. But then there's my expenses and my time, to say nothing of the inconvenience and loss of face. And there's the expense of sussing the job, setting up the alibis, the transport, paying the muscle, and the overheads. And it all comes to a tidy sum. What's left for me to do? Somebody's got to pay. Well, who caused all this to happen? Your son did. So common sense and logic says he's the one to pay for it. Right?'

Piggott pursed his lips. 'I don't know,' he said.

'Well tell me, Cecil. Have *you* got thirteen thousand pounds?'

Piggott blew out a lungful of air. 'Wow. Maybe he didn't expect the cost to be so high.'

'I think you're looking for the two-letter word "no".'

'Thirteen thousand pounds?' Piggott said. 'Is that the value you put on a man's life?'

'No. That's what I would have earned on that last job if your son had kept his part of the bargain. But now, friend, I've had enough of this. Your time is up.' He turned back to the piano and called out towards the door. 'Take him away, Mr Crum. He's beginning to annoy me.'

Crum grabbed the man's arms. 'Right, pal. Let's go.'

Piggott struggled with the heavy. He didn't want to leave before he had said his piece. 'Just a minute. *Just a minute!*' he protested. 'If I can get you the money, will you leave my son alone?'

'Huh. And where are you going to get that sort of money from, hmm? Now, I'm a very busy man. Goodbye.'

Crum squeezed Piggott's forearms. 'Let's go.'

The pain made him wince. 'If you could call off your gorilla, I honestly believe I can.'

'Hold the muscle,' the man at the piano said. 'Right, Cecil. You honestly think you can? Well, there's a laugh. I don't know. You *honestly* think you can. Hmm. I tell you what, friend, I'll do a deal with you. I know I'm stupid and soft, but I just can't help myself. It'll be my downfall. If you give me thirteen thousand pounds in cash *before* we find your son, I'll consider the debt paid.'

'And you'll leave him in peace?'

'Yes. But if in the meantime we find him, my conscience and my principles won't let me do anything other than put out his lights, *permanently*. You understand that, Cecil? And it has to be used English currency, not consecutive numbers, and not funny money, you understand?' He called across to Crum. 'Take him away. And I don't want to see him ever again unless he is seriously loaded with moolah. All right?'

'I'll get it,' Piggott said. 'You'll see.'

'One more thing, Cecil. I like to execute my business deals in privacy. I don't like it much when I make any concession that it gets broadcast to the fuzz, and their size tens and elevens trample over all my Axminster. And they speak with such dreadful grammar — split infinitives all over the shop. No finesse, you understand? No finesse. And to save face I have to permanently shut the mouths that open too much. Understand?'

'I understand,' Piggott said.

The man at the piano smiled. 'I like you, Cecil, I do. Not enough that if you didn't honour your promise I'd let you live. No. But still . . .'

Piggott's insides shuddered and he felt very cold, but he didn't want the man to see how scared he was.

'When I get this money . . . how . . . how do I contact you?'

'Simple. There's a Chinese restaurant on Hope Street.'

Piggott remembered it as the Can Can Club. It got closed down. Lost its licence. The strippers did more than strip. For years before that it was a working men's club.

'I know it,' he said.

'Leave a message with Wang. He works there.'

Piggott nodded. 'And who shall I say the message is for?'

'The piano player. It'll get to me.' He jerked his head towards the door, indicating to Crum that he should take the prisoner away.

'Right, boss,' the heavy said, then led Piggott out of the room and closed the door.

The man at the piano was alone again and he began tapping out the three notes. Then he stopped. 'And I was really getting to like him. That's the trouble with me, I'm a real softie at heart. It's not a useful quality to foster. Can cost me a lot of moolah. Oh, dear me, no.'

TWO

DI Angel's office
Bromersley Police Station, South Yorkshire
Monday, 11 November, 8.35 a.m.

Detective Inspector Michael Angel was in his office writing out his expenses when he became aware of the buzzing of an insect overhead. He threw down his pen and looked above him at the little black creature flitting hither and thither round the light bulb. He quickly looked across his desk for something to swat it with. There was nothing but paper, pen and a ruler. He snatched up the ruler and swiped at it, missing each time. The tatty vellum lampshade looked even tattier and the fly responded by buzzing at a higher volume.

The phone rang.

He threw the ruler on the desk and picked up the phone.

'Angel,' he said.

It was the woman on the police station switchboard. 'Ah, Inspector, I've got an urgent call for the super but he's out. Will you take it? It's from Special Branch. It's a woman. Wouldn't give her name.'

'Of course,' Angel said. 'Put her through.'

'You're through.'

'DI Angel speaking. Who is this?'

'Good morning, Inspector. This is DS Seeley of Special Branch,' she said. 'This is an official unofficial notice. In the course of our enquiries it has been revealed that a man living in your area is on a hit list. We understand that he's a scrap metal dealer by the name of Cecil Piggott. That's all I can tell you.'

Angel wrinkled his nose. It was a phone call he would rather have not received. 'Thank you, ma'am,' he said and replaced the phone.

He turned to his computer and tapped in the name. He was pleased to see that the man had not served time nor ever been charged.

He picked up the phone and tapped in the number for the station sergeant, DS Clifton, the oldest serving policeman at Bromersley police station.

'Bernie, ever heard of a Cecil Piggott, scrap metal dealer?'

'Not been through our hands as far as I can recall, sir. But he has a son we want to clear up several offences, mostly to do with the taking of motor vehicles.'

'Oh yes,' Angel said. 'Arthur Piggott. Got the makings of a real hoodlum, that lad has. It's time he was caught and charged. Thank you, Bernie.'

He replaced the phone.

* * *

A few minutes later he was in his car with DS Flora Carter driving down Doncaster Road to Cecil Piggott's scrap metal yard. The big wooden gates were open so he drove straight in, manoeuvring between piles of damaged cars stacked six or seven high, oil drums, old domestic ovens and fridges, to reach the far end, where there was a small brick-built office.

Angel stopped the car and they got out. It was a muddy yard and they had to pick their way through the puddles. The office door was open and a man of about fifty came through onto the wooden decking.

When he saw Angel and Flora he didn't look pleased. He sniffed and said, 'You're coppers, aren't you?'

'We are indeed,' Angel said. 'Just a friendly call. Are you Mr Piggott?

'Yes, that's me. You'd better come in then, I suppose. Your lads were only here last week though — what on earth do you want now? They had a good look at my stock and my books and they said everything was all right. I do object to this carry-on all the time.'

Angel and Carter stepped onto the wooden decking and into the tiny office.

Angel said, 'We are here in *your* interest, Mr Piggott.'

Piggott assumed a bored expression. 'Huh, I doubt *that*,' he said.

'It's true,' Flora said.

Angel said, 'Mr Piggott, you are on a hit list. Somebody means to murder you.'

Piggott smiled. 'Somebody means to murder *me*? Where have you got that from?'

'Passed on from Special Branch. You can rely on them.'

Piggott continued smiling. He shook his head.

Angel said, 'So you need to take the appropriate precautions. Have you any idea who it might be?'

12

'No,' Piggott said. 'Sometimes I get a customer who accepts an offer I make for his scrap, whatever it might be, and when he goes into the pub, he meets somebody who reckons he knows somebody who would have given him more. So the customer thinks he's been done. He comes back here and tries to negotiate the deal all over again. He might get a bit angry but I wouldn't expect he would want to murder me.'

'Well, I would shut up shop for a few weeks,' Angel said. 'Until it all blows over.'

Flora said, 'Take a holiday. Go away.'

'A long way away,' Angel said.

Piggott pulled a face. 'I can't shut the shop. This shop hasn't been shut for nigh on fifteen years, and that was because I had to have my appendix out. Besides, we don't like holidays. Wife won't fly and I can't eat that foreign muck.'

Angel and Flora exchanged glances.

'You've got a son, haven't you?' Angel said cunningly. The inspector would have loved to have felt Piggott's collar.

'Yes. Arthur. So what?'

'Couldn't he take over the business for a short while?'

'No. He doesn't know anything about scrap.'

'Where does he live?'

'Dunno. He always seems to be on the move.'

Angel wasn't surprised. There were several charges on the books against him.

'If he lived a distance away,' Angel said, 'I was going to suggest that maybe you and your wife could stay with him.'

Piggott shook his head. 'I don't know where he lives.'

'Well, you see him from time to time, don't you?'

'Huh. Only when he needs money. So *you* don't know who it is that wants to murder me?'

'No, we don't,' Angel said. 'It was just a tip-off. If we knew anything more I would tell you.'

Piggott wrinkled his nose and then shook his head.

Angel realised that he was not taking the threat seriously. 'Your life is in danger, Mr Piggott. This is not a rumour. This is real. The information we have is that someone out there intends to murder you. And if you don't do something about it he will succeed. If we had enough men, I would put a couple of armed guards on duty twenty-four-seven, but we haven't. At least you could protect yourself and disappear for a month or so.'

'It'll take more than an anonymous threat to bother me.'

* * *

'A complete waste of time and breath,' Angel muttered to himself as he put his trilby on the hook on the side of the stationery cupboard in his office.

He sat down at his desk and returned to writing up his expenses when there was an urgent knock on the door followed by it being thrown open by Cadet Cassandra Jagger noisily banging against a chair.

'Steady on,' Angel said, looking up.

Cassie, as she was known, was only seventeen, and eager to be detective.

She stood there, her face scarlet and her eyes wide. 'Excuse me, sir. But you'll never guess who is in reception asking for you.'

Angel threw down his pen and turned his head. 'Cassie, how many times have I told you? Don't burst in here like somebody's thrust a shovel full of red-hot coals down the back of your pants.'

'Yes, sir. I mean no, sir.'

'Who is it then? The Pope? The Queen? Is this a guessing game?'

'It's only Lisa Maria Gooden,' she said, and began to clap her hands together silently and jump up and down.

'If she's a pop star, I wouldn't know her.'

'She's a film star, sir. She played the slave girl who married the old man of the woods out of pity . . . who then turned into a prince in that blockbuster that just won six Oscars. Her husband, Miles Persimmon, an absolute genius, produced it. He must have cabinets full of Oscars.'

Angel frowned, then glared at her still jumping up and down and clapping her hands together.

She stopped, smiled and shook her head. 'I'm so excited. You *must* have heard of them. Fabulously wealthy. Have a house near here . . . well it's a farm, near Tunistone.'

'What does she want?'

'I don't know, sir. She asked to see you. She's in the waiting room.'

'Right, Cassie, better show her in.'

Two minutes later, she arrived with the actress.

'Miss Gooden, this is Detective Inspector Angel.'

Angel looked up at the actress, blinked and stood up. He was greatly impressed as he looked over the pencil-slim woman with the small, pretty mouth and high cheekbones.

'Good morning, Inspector Angel,' she said.

He couldn't speak for a minute. He was too busy taking everything in.

She was wearing a plain, well-cut red silk dress and a cream-coloured summer coat. She carried a small handbag. Diamonds in the clasp caught the light and reflected on her and the office ceiling. Angel noticed an aura of French perfume.

They shook hands. Her hand was small, moist and cold.

'Good morning,' he said and gestured to a chair.

She sat down.

He looked across at Cassie by the door and with a jerk of the head instructed her to leave. Her face showed her disappointment.

She turned, went out and closed the door.

'Now, Miss Gooden, what can I do for you?' Angel said.

'Are you the Mountie, the detective inspector who always gets his man?'

Angel was a little embarrassed by this nickname — erroneously awarded to him years ago by an eager journalist who wanted a good headline.

'I have that honour, Miss Gooden, although it is not exactly fair on the many other detectives who also work hard to get their man.'

'Good, I have the right detective,' she said. 'Mr Angel, I will come straight to the point. I have been married five years to Miles Persimmon. I am his second wife. His first wife died tragically young of heart failure. It has been a mostly happy experience: a partnership making blockbuster movies where we have hardly ever been apart. But then suddenly we find ourselves incompatible. Being together is boring and uncomfortable. On my husband's part, I have to say, even hateful. So much so that he has coolly told me that after he returns from a business trip to Ireland, he intends to murder me. I know that may seem outrageous, but I am sure that he means to do this himself and furthermore, that nobody will prove anything against him. He *can* do this. I don't know how, but he is a very clever man. He will do it unless a cleverer brain can stop him.'

Angel blinked. That sounded like a challenge if ever there was one. He rubbed his chin. He didn't know this woman. It was difficult for him to take literally all that she had said.

'Are you sure your husband is serious, Miss Gooden?' Angel said. 'Sometimes pretty appalling things are exchanged during a heated row or a disagreement. It can happen within a marriage.'

'That's true, Inspector, but I have never said that I was going to murder him. Besides, he has never said anything he didn't mean, and he always seems to have full control over everything he says and does. Not like me. I can blow my top at anything and anybody if I'm wound up enough.'

Angel knew the feeling and, looking at her beneath the glamour and the make-up, he thought that she probably had a very short fuse. He wondered whether this was a simple domestic row that really didn't need his involvement.

'Has your husband committed any crime like this previously — or indeed has he been in trouble with the police at all?'

'Not at all,' she said. Her voice suddenly changed. 'You don't believe me, do you?' She looked downwards and put her fingers to her mouth.

'I don't *disbelieve* you, Miss Gooden. It is just . . . erm . . . difficult to understand. A murderer doesn't usually announce his criminal intention . . . and so openly.'

'If you knew him, you wouldn't think it difficult at all,' she said.

Angel turned to his computer, brought up the Police National Computer website and tapped in Miles Persimmon. He turned to her and asked, 'Did your husband ever use any other name?'

'No,' she said.

Angel tapped a key, and the browser showed him a completely blank sheet.

He turned to the distraught actress. 'You'll be pleased to know that your husband is not on our books.'

Her eyes flashed. 'I already told you that,' she said. 'What are you going to do? Wait until he murders me and then arrest him?'

'Miss Gooden, the threat to kill is incredibly difficult to prove. Do you have any witnesses to this?'

Lisa's face muscles tightened.

'I didn't think it would be this difficult to get help,' she said.

Angel pursed his lips for a second. 'Amid this dreadful statement to you, Miss Gooden, what do you think motivated him to even mention something as mundane as a business trip to Ireland?'

'I don't know, Inspector. All I can say is that he's a tidy man, over-organised if that's possible . . . and terribly, horribly frightening.'

'Where can I see Mr Persimmon?' Angel asked.

'When I left he was at the farm. He has an office there.'

'I need to see him.'

'Won't do any good.'

'But you don't have any objection?'

'No. You can try.'

Angel sighed. 'If we had the manpower and the time, I would appoint armed constables to be with you twenty-four-seven. But as it is . . .'

'Look, Inspector Angel, it's no good telling me what you *can't* do. Tell me what you *can* do.'

'With the information you have supplied and the fact that you cannot support it with any evidence, I can do nothing.

But there's something you can do for yourself and I very much urge you to do it.'

'What's that? I must do something.'

'Well, you should change your looks. Dye your hair. Leave off the make-up. Wear relatively sober clothes. And change your name. Tell nobody. Pack a suitcase, and using public transport go to a place you have never been to before. Choose private, self-catering accommodation, not a five-star luxury hotel with room service. Move every seven to ten days and stay somewhere else. Pay for everything with cash. And do not contact, phone or write to anyone you know. In other words, disappear. Keep this up until the danger has gone.'

Lisa put her head in her hands and sighed. 'Mr Angel, you must be out of your mind. I am a world-renowned actress. And, although I say so myself, something of a leader in fashion. Wherever there is a cinema or a computer in the world the people will know me. I have been a face on their screens repeatedly the last six or seven years. Even if I shaved off my hair and painted my body with woad I would still be recognised. Besides, looking good is my business. I have a life to live, a career to follow. I am at the top now. I still have my daily gym sessions to keep up, a strict diet to follow, fan mail to deal with. Offers of work come flowing in . . . Your suggestion is stupid. Impractical. Impossible. Frankly, it is a ridiculous proposal.'

'I thought you wanted to stay alive, Miss Gooden? The lifestyle I am recommending wouldn't be forever.'

She stood up. Her face was scarlet, her chest heaving. 'I can see that I am wasting my time.'

Unmoved, Angel said, 'Miss Gooden, believe me, if you have told me the truth and you want to stay alive, disappearing for a month or two in the way I have prescribed is the only way.'

In his BMW, Angel followed Lisa Maria Gooden in her chauffeur-driven Daimler up to Tunistone, through black wrought-iron gates, down a long drive, through trees, bushes and grass to the gravelled frontage of the farmhouse, passing the farm gate that separated the house from the farm buildings.

Angel met up with Miss Gooden at the front door. A liveried maid let them in, took Angel's trilby and put it on the hall table.

Miss Gooden checked with the maid that her husband was still in his office, then turned to Angel and, pointing to a partly open door at the end of the hall, in a hushed voice said, 'He's in there.'

Angel nodded and made his way down to the office. He knocked on the door, pushing it open to reveal Miles Persimmon at his desk, writing.

He looked up, frowned and said, 'Who the hell are you?' He quickly followed on with, 'Never mind. Go away. I'm busy.'

Persimmon continued writing.

Angel took out his ID and badge, held it up for the man to see and walked towards the desk.

Persimmon glanced upwards. His lips tightened. 'I didn't invite you in.'

Angel was undeterred. 'I'm DI Angel, Mr Persimmon. I need to talk to you for a few minutes.'

Persimmon resumed writing. 'Make an appointment with my secretary in the next room,' he said. 'And close the door on your way out. Good day.'

'It's about your wife, Mr Persimmon.'

'I thought it would be. I have no time just now. *See* my secretary.'

'Your wife says that you have threatened to kill her.'

Persimmon threw down his pen, sighed and said, 'Look here, Mr Angel. My wife is nuts. On Saturday night I returned from a tiring first-night showing of a film that I have produced and directed, hotly tipped for awards season. I have to tidy up all the loose ends — promotion, distribution, marketing — and I am in the throes of producing and directing another masterpiece. My presence is required in Ireland the day after tomorrow with some of my staff to settle on locations, which means I am weeks behind in my private life as well as my business life. Now will you please go away and let me catch up with it?'

He pulled the silver flask from his pocket, took a swig and replaced it.

'I want to talk to you briefly about your *wife*,' Angel said.

'So you said.'

'You have threatened to kill her.'

'Yes, and I'm sure I will given half the chance, but I have other things to see to before I can get to that.'

Angel's eyebrows shot up and his heart began to beat a little faster. 'You're treating the murder very lightly,' he said.

'I haven't time to talk about that now. I have politely invited you to make an appointment with my secretary.'

'Do you realise that if your wife was found dead in the near future, I would know it was you who had murdered her, and you would go to prison for not less than twenty-five years?'

'You would have to prove it first, Mr Angel, and *that* you would never do.'

Angel's jaw muscle tightened. He recognised the challenge but hoped it would never happen.

'I wouldn't push your luck, Mr Persimmon,' he said heavily.

'Luck is not in my vocabulary. Now I suggest you go, or I will report to your superior that you are harassing a perfectly respectable and innocent citizen.'

'I am not harassing you. Just doing my job. I could always get a warrant. And you are *not* an innocent citizen.'

Persimmon closed his eyes and ran his hand through his hair. 'Well, for God's sake, go and get one then.'

THREE

Angel pulled open a drawer in the desk and took out his address book. He found a number and tapped it into the phone.

A man with a musical Irish accent answered. 'Garda Central Dublin. Can I help you?'

'This is DI Angel, Bromersley police, UK. I want to speak with Captain Harrigan, please.'

'Hold on then there, sir, if you please.'

There was a short pause and then a warm voice said, 'Hello. Patrick Harrigan here. Long time since I heard from you, Michael.'

They reminisced about several villains they had both been jointly investigating in years past and the few bottles of Jameson's they had had the pleasure of drinking in celebration of the results, before Angel got round to the purpose of his call.

He told Captain Harrigan about the situation that Lisa Maria Gooden had disclosed to him and the interview he had subsequently had with her husband, Miles Persimmon. Then Angel said, 'I have just heard from the wife, Lisa, that her husband intends to meet up with several members of his staff at Dublin airport to search for locations in Ireland for a new film he's making. Now, I'm surmising that at some point Persimmon will double back to Bromersley to murder her, then return to Ireland, having created some sort of clever, so-called unbreakable alibi that shows him to be conspicuously involved in something over there with a thousand witnesses present at the time of the crime.'

'Ah, Michael, I understand. One of those clever devils. And you want me to monitor his whereabouts and advise you if he leaves the country.'

'Precisely that,' Angel said.

'A pleasure, Michael. No problem at all. Just you let me know what flight he's on and wire me a photograph of him.'

* * *

Customs Examiner's Office, Dublin Airport
Wednesday, 13 November, 10.30 a.m.

The door opened and a customs officer in uniform entered, followed by Miles Persimmon and Captain Harrigan in plain clothes.

Persimmon looked around the small office. His eyes were bright with anger, his jaw set, his fists clenched. He glared and said, 'I've no time for all this, I tell you. You're going to look the biggest fool in the world when you find out who I am.'

'We know who you *say* you are, sir,' Harrigan said. 'You're Miles Persimmon, a film producer. You're here to make a film.'

'That's right,' Persimmon said. 'It's the truth.'

'And I asked you if it was an Irish story. And you — face-tiously, I expect — said, no, Egyptian. I asked you its title and you said there isn't one yet. I asked you who was in it and you said you didn't know that either! What am I to think?'

Persimmon's face went scarlet. 'I explained all that,' he bawled.

'Now, come over here, sir. Empty your pockets onto this table.'

Persimmon didn't budge. 'I will do nothing of the sort. I want to see my solicitor.'

'Oh yes, sir,' Harrigan said. 'And the Garda fully recog-nises your right, sir. Who are we calling?'

The captain reached out for the phone.

'David Hooper. He's in London. Partner in the firm Bracegirdle and Hooper.'

Harrigan looked across at him and slowly shook his head. 'It's a long way to come, sir. Your solicitor might not be able to get here until tomorrow at the earliest. We would have to hold you in a cell overnight. I wouldn't recommend that, sir.'

Persimmon realised the truth of what the policeman had said. His face contorted in frustrated anger. He hesitated a moment or two then finally made up his mind. He crossed to the table.

Harrigan returned the phone to its holster.

Persimmon slowly and deliberately emptied his pockets, starting with the top one. When he had finished, he said, 'That's it.'

The customs officer took up a position behind the table and cursorily looked over the contents. 'Will you please take off your jacket?'

Persimmon froze. 'What for?'

'What do you think?' Harrigan said. 'He wants to check the weave and make sure there are no concealed secret messages to you from the Kremlin.'

Persimmon glared at him.

The customs officer smiled. 'It won't take five minutes, sir.'

Persimmon shrugged, loudly breathed out and took off the jacket. He passed it to the officer, who held it at arm's length and left the room.

In the next office a man was seated at the ready, holding a pair of small scissors. He took the jacket, cut several stitches at the hem between the lining and the jacket material, opened it up an inch or so, then the customs officer passed him a tiny transmitter fixed to double-sided adhesive tape. The man carefully put it through the opening and pressed it hard against the jacket material. He then sewed up the small opening, cut the cotton and handed the jacket back to the customs officer. This was all executed in silence and at great speed.

The customs officer nodded, returned to the examination room and handed the jacket back to Persimmon.

'That's all right, sir,' the customs officer said.

Persimmon sniffed in acknowledgement, snatched back the jacket and put it on.

The desk phone began to ring. The customs officer picked it up and looked knowingly at Harrigan. 'It's a call from the Met for you.'

Harrigan took the phone. 'Hello. Captain Harrigan speaking.'

An Irish voice said, 'Ah. Yes, sir. We thought you'd like to know that that transmitter just fitted into that gent's jacket is sending out a signal as clear and as sweet as the lovely Dana.'

'Oh. Thank you, sir,' Harrigan said into the mouthpiece. Then he surreptitiously pressed the off button but continued speaking into the phone. 'You can confirm everything? . . . And we can drop all further investigations and release Mr Persimmon immediately? . . . Right, sir.'

Harrigan returned the phone to its holster on the desk.

He looked across at Persimmon. 'You've been cleared, sir. We apologise for any inconvenience caused. You are free to go.'

Persimmon jumped up and made for the door. Then he stopped, turned and glared at Harrigan. 'I should bloody well think so. You haven't heard the last of this.'

The door slammed.

Harrigan smiled. 'And good luck with the film.'

* * *

Piggott's scrap metal yard
Doncaster Road, Bromersley, South Yorkshire
Friday, 15 November, 8 a.m.

A black limousine with shaded windows pulled up outside the open gate of Piggott's scrap metal yard.

'This is the place, boss,' the driver said.

From the back of the limousine a slim man in a smart suit, overcoat, fedora and brown-and-white leather shoes put his hand inside his overcoat to his holster and pulled out a Walther PP semi-automatic. He looked at it, smiled and returned it to its holster.

'Keep the engine running, Mr Crum,' the man said to the driver sotto voce. 'This won't take long.'

He slipped out of the car, walked through the open gate and made his way through the tall heaps of scrap towards the office at the other end. It had been raining most of the night, making the track into a wet and muddy mess. The man picked his way carefully and raised his trousers at the creases several centimetres to save them from becoming dirty. He wasn't pleased when he saw that his shoes had become spattered with mud.

He reached the wooden decking and looked round to see if there was anything he could use to wipe his shoes clean, but there was nothing.

Cecil Piggott was at his desk in his tiny office sorting through some bills that were coming up to be paid.

He heard footsteps on the decking. He spun round in the swivel chair then stood up to see the man standing in the office doorway.

The man pulled out the Walther, released the safety catch and directed it at Piggott's stomach. He gripped the gun so tightly that his hand was waving about uncertainly.

Piggott sucked in a lungful of air. His heart thumped through his shirt.

He could see that the man's face was full of anger and hatred and that his breathing was irregular.

'You called in the fuzz, Cecil,' he said. 'After all that rabbiting about you keeping your trap shut to them and yet . . . you squealed to the fuzz.'

Piggott blinked several times as he looked down the barrel of the gun. 'I didn't. I don't know how they knew. This copper came here. He said that he had had reliable information that I was on a hit list somewhere.'

'What hit list was that?'

'I don't know.'

'You don't know. Who supplied the reliable information?'

'I don't know.'

'You don't know. You don't know nothing. You squealed to the fuzz and you didn't come back to me with the moolah.'

'I couldn't raise it, but I didn't tell the police *anything*.'

'You're a liar, Cecil. And not a very good one. But you won't tell anymore lies.'

'It's the truth, I tell you—'

The man wrinkled his nose. His staring eyes grew wide. He fired three shots in quick succession.

Piggott fell back into the chair. He flopped there motionless, like a sack of potatoes.

The man then glanced round the room, stuffed the Walther into the holster and walked quickly back through the yard, ignoring the puddles, to the waiting limousine. The wheels began to move the moment the man opened the door.

* * *

Bromersley Police Station, South Yorkshire
Friday, 15 November, 8.28 a.m.

As Angel made his way down the long green corridor to his office, he could hear the phone on his desk ringing out. He threw open the office door, reached over the desk and picked up the handset.

It was Sergeant Clifton on the station reception desk.

'I thought you'd be in, sir. I had a 999 call at 8.16 a.m. from a Mrs Piggott. She was in a bit of a state.'

Angel slumped down in his swivel chair and tightened the grip he had on the phone as he dreaded what he was certain was coming next.

'She said that she had found her husband shot dead in the office in his scrapyard,' the sergeant said.

Angel was dazed. He felt a cold heavy lump in his chest.

He was thinking . . . He should have done more to save the man's life. But what? Did he do enough to make Piggott take the threat seriously?

'Are you still there, sir?' Clifton said.

'Er . . . yes,' he said. 'Yes, Bernie.'

Angel knew it was not the time to analyse the situation. He had to carry on as usual and not allow anyone to realise the turmoil within his mind.

'I sent Echo Charlie One.'

'Right, Bernie,' he said. 'I'm on my way.'

Angel replaced the phone, took a very deep breath and walked across the corridor to the general office. Looking round the door jamb, he saw DS Carter at her desk and jerked his head, indicating that he wanted her to come with him.

They took his car. He said very little on the journey other than that they were to attend a murder scene and the name of the victim.

A few seconds elapsed, then Flora blinked and looked at Angel. 'That was the man we were warned was on a hit list . . . the Special Branch tip-off . . .'

Angel nodded and pushed the gear stick into top.

Flora sighed. 'Oh, sir.'

A few more seconds passed.

'Oh, sir. That's simply awful. And he didn't take it seriously . . .'

Again Angel nodded.

There was another pause in the conversation.

'Well, we did what we could,' she said. 'We told him it was a serious warning. You made several suggestions as to how he could hide away, but he didn't want to know. He simply *didn't want to know*.'

'We didn't do enough, Flora. There should have been a way to force him to close the yard and go away.'

'We couldn't *force* him, sir. This is supposed to be a free country. But we could have arrested him on some trumped-up charge.'

'We couldn't do that either. We can't *break* the law to *keep* the law.'

Arriving at the scrapyard, they found the big gates open. The lights on the sign board were still on even though the sun was shining. Angel stopped the BMW on the road and they walked through the gates into the yard. He looked backwards and frowned. 'Close and secure these gates, Flora. I expect there'll be bolts on the inside.'

'Right, sir.'

He walked on the ground between the heaps of crashed cars, bedsteads, assorted oil drums and metal piping up to a stationary police car. It was in front of the small office.

PC Sean Donohue, patrolman and driver of Echo Charlie One, came out of the office and saluted. 'Morning, sir.'

Angel braced himself. He pointed to the gates behind them. 'I've told DS Carter to secure the gates. I don't want any more marks on the ground. We will be checking the ground for tyre prints.'

'I wondered whether to drive in, sir, but—'

'I know, Sean. It could have been an emergency. Well, lead on. Show me the victim.'

He followed Donohue up onto the wooden decking and the patrolman gestured towards the open door of the tiny office.

'Was this door open?' Angel said.

'Yes, sir. It's just as I found it. Haven't touched a thing.'

Angel went inside.

The white-faced corpse of Cecil Piggott was slumped in the swivel office chair, which was turned away from the desk and facing the door. His eyes were closed and his mouth was slightly open. There was an area as big as a dinner plate of congealed blood down the front of his shirt. The smell of gunpowder was still in the air.

Angel stood there, touching nothing, his eagle eyes searching everywhere: the tidy desk . . . the phone . . . the wooden floorboards . . . the stark unadorned brick walls . . . the small fan heater . . .

He came out, his head down, his lips pursed. His eyes made only tiny movements, blinking frequently in thought. Angel had seen hundreds of dead bodies in his time, but this one was disturbing his equilibrium more than most — probably due to the fact that he had been in Cecil Piggott's company in that little office only four days ago.

Carter came up to him.

'Flora, tell Don Taylor I want him to take casts of anything he can in the scrapyard. There are quite a lot of sharp tyre marks and shoe prints that might lead us somewhere. And when the doc has finished, tell Scrivens to get Cecil Piggott's mobile and check his calls for the last month.'

'Will do,' she said, scribbling in her notebook.

Then he gestured to the office door. 'Better take a look, Flora. It's not pleasant, but it stiffens your resolve to find and lock up the murderer.'

Her eyes flashed in panic. She took a sharp intake of breath, exhaled slowly and tentatively approached the office door.

Donohue approached Angel from a path behind the office. 'Dr Mac's here, sir,' he said. 'So is DS Taylor from SOCO and his team. They were holding back for you.'

'Right, Sean, let them get on with it,' Angel said. 'Didn't Mrs Piggott find the victim?'

'She did. Are you ready to see her now?'

'I am. Where is she?'

'In the house,' Donohue said. 'Follow me, sir.'

The patrolman led Angel through a white picket gate behind the office and along the garden path of a small detached house to the side door.

'There's a doorbell somewhere, sir.'

Angel found the doorbell and pressed it.

'Thank you, Sean,' Angel said.

'I'll go and tell them you've finished, sir,' Donohue said and dashed off.

As Angel waited, he noticed Dr Mac's car and SOCO's van parked on the street behind Doncaster Road.

The door was eventually opened by a slim woman in her forties. Not at all what Angel had expected for the wife of a scrap dealer.

Angel blinked, introduced himself and showed his ID and police badge.

'You'll be the investigating officer, Inspector?' the woman said, her face still white with shock.

'Yes. I would like to ask you a few questions, Mrs Piggott . . . if it's convenient?'

'Please come in,' she said and closed the door, leading him into a sitting room.

Angel said, 'I appreciate no time is ever convenient for a woman to answer questions about the murder of her husband.'

'Please sit down, Inspector,' she said. 'There's no time like the present. Let's get it over with. And please, call me Amy.'

Angel sat down in the easy chair. He didn't want to call her Amy but he didn't want to seem superior either.

'Tell me, what exactly happened?'

'I was at the gym. I go most mornings. I usually go about seven. I do about an hour. When I got back, I didn't know Cecil had got up and gone down to the office. I called upstairs to tell him I was back and to come down for breakfast. Eventually, when he didn't reply, I went up to see . . . of course, he wasn't there. I thought he must be in the office in the yard. So I rang the office — there's a phone extension down there. Again, no reply. I began to get a bit worried. It wasn't like him. So I . . .'

She stopped. Bit her lip and turned away.

Angel thought that she was exercising as much control over her emotions as she could manage.

'Take your time. I know it's difficult.'

Without turning around, she nodded.

A few moments later, she turned back. 'So, I went down to the office and . . . I saw . . . I saw my Cecil . . .'

'Did you go into the office?' Angel said.

'No need to. No . . . I came away quickly. Came back here . . . dialled 999 . . . phoned the police.'

'Have you any idea who might be responsible for this?'

'No.'

'Did you see any vehicle or person around — someone you were perhaps unhappy about?'

'No.'

'Has anything out of the ordinary happened to you or your husband recently?'

'No.'

'Have you had any threats or foreknowledge that your husband was in any kind of danger?'

'No.'

Angel was surprised that Cecil Piggott had apparently not told his wife anything about the threat passed on by Special Branch that he was on a hit list. Angel decided that he wasn't going to tell her, although it may have to come out at the inquest.

'Which gym do you go to?' he asked.

'The one in town. Bromersley Central. Been going there for years. Only ten minutes in the car.'

'Cecil appears to have been shot in the chest. Did you hear gunshots?'

'No. I assume it happened while I was at the gym.'

'What time did you leave for the gym and what time did you return?'

'I left about ten minutes to seven, worked out for about an hour, left at eight and got back for about ten past eight.'

'Have you a recent photograph of your husband we could borrow?'

'Yes. I'll sort one out for you before you go.'

'Thank you. Now one last thing for now. A practical matter. Are you going to be all right on your own?'

She sighed and tried to smile, then said, 'Well, I'll soon find out, won't I?'

'You've a son, Arthur, haven't you?' Angel asked slyly. 'Could he come and stay with you for a while?'

She shrugged. 'I don't know.'

'Where does he live?'

She hesitated. 'His work takes him all over. He doesn't have a permanent address.'

'Can you contact him? I would like to ask him some questions.'

'No. I wish I could. He would be such a comfort to me. And he adored his father . . . He visits us every couple of months or so. He'll be devastated when he hears. Oh my god!' she said, then there were more sobs.

'Thank you, Mrs Piggott,' Angel said. 'That's all I need for now.'

FOUR

Several hours later, there was a knock on Angel's office door.

'Come in,' he said.

The white-haired figure of a man with a bag came in. It was Dr Mac, the Home Office pathologist and a good friend of Angel.

'Hi there, Doc,' Angel said. 'Glad you came. Sit down. What you got?'

Mac shook his head. 'Not a lot.'

Angel sighed. 'One day, Mac, you'll come here and you'll tell me not only what time the victim died, but also who did it, how he did it, where he did it, the motive and the precise place where I can arrest him.'

'And one day,' the old doctor said, 'I shall be relaxing on a golf course having scored a hole in one and about to sweep the board with the chief constable, and I shall *not* be interrupted by a phone call requiring my urgent presence somewhere.'

Angel smiled. 'I'm sorry, Mac. Just hopeful, I guess.'

'Well, like I said, I haven't got much,' Mac said. 'He died from three shots to the chest. It looks as though the murderer was standing quite close to the victim . . . there was a lot of powder . . . say, six to eight feet.'

'Suggests that the murderer knew Piggott,' Angel said. 'Or at least trusted him to come so close. Unless he thought it was a customer, of course.'

'Time of death . . . between seven and eight this morning.'

Angel frowned. 'That's early for a murder.'

'I understand you had a tip-off?'

Angel pulled a disagreeable face. 'Yes,' he said. 'He wasn't murdered in the heat of the moment. It was planned. Sounded like an organised gang execution. And I don't like the thought that we have a gang of tooled-up heavies congregating in Bromersley — we're not prepared to deal with it. We haven't any armed men here, so we have to draw from Wakefield, and that all takes time.'

Dr Mac stood up and reached for his bag.

'Is that it then, Mac?'

'Afraid so, Michael. Be in touch if anything comes up at the post-mortem.'

* * *

DI Angel's office
Bromersley Police Station, South Yorkshire
Monday, 25 November, 11.30 a.m.

It had been ten days since the murder of Cecil Piggott, and little progress had been made in discovering the culprit. Angel had been investigating every possible suspect but had not yet made a breakthrough, nor had he caught the fly that from time to time buzzed annoyingly around his office.

Angel was standing by his desk, tightly gripping a rolled-up copy of the *Sun* in his hand. He was looking round and listening for the fly, which had suddenly become silent and was presumably resting in its secret hiding place.

There was a knock at the door and DS Carter came in.

'Ah, Flora,' Angel said as he tossed the paper onto his desk. 'Anything fresh on the Piggott case?'

She shook her head. 'No, sir, and it's his funeral tomorrow.'

Angel rubbed his chin roughly.

'Yes, I know. I've been thinking about that,' he said, his eyes narrowing. 'Find Crisp for me, pronto.'

Carter rushed off.

Angel sat down and waited a moment, tapping his fingers on the desk top, then swiftly reached out for the phone. 'Bernie,' he said, 'is anyone using the detection van?'

'No, sir.'

'Right. I want it cleaned up and prepared for a job tomorrow morning.'

'Right, sir,' Bernie said.

Angel replaced the phone.

The door opened and in came DS Trevor Crisp.

Angel looked up. 'Crisp, drop whatever you're working on and check over that fancy new video camera. I want it to film the face of every man, woman, child and villain that goes to Cecil Piggott's funeral tomorrow. Bernie is seeing to the van.'

'I can't, sir,' Crisp said. 'I have an appointment with Duggie Lampton's probation officer at—'

Angel sucked in a quick breath of air and blinked at Crisp. 'Duggie Lampton's probation officer? Well cancel it. Pickpockets can wait. This is a murder investigation.'

Crisp's mouth dropped open. 'But—'

The phone rang.

Angel jerked his head towards the door to tell Crisp to leave. Crisp pulled a sour face and stomped out of the office as Angel reached out for the phone. 'DI Angel.'

He knew it was Detective Superintendent Horace Harker on the phone because he always cleared his throat with a double-barrelled cough before he spoke. Harker was Angel's boss and responsible for the day-to-day running of Bromersley police station.

'Come up here straightaway — I want an update,' the man said and put down the handset.

Angel wrinkled his nose, made his way up the corridor to the last door but one, tapped on it and entered.

The office was untidy and overheated and smelled of menthol. It was always like that.

Detective Superintendent Harker was not immediately visible. He was seated at his desk behind several piles of letters, files, reports, books and boxes of pills and bottles of medicine or ointment. In boring moments, Angel tried to read the labels of some of them. There were pills for arthritis, headaches, coughs and colds, diarrhoea, constipation, haemorrhoids, gout . . . and complaints he could neither pronounce nor spell.

Harker's head was the shape of a turnip. He was mostly bald but had a collar of white hair the shape of a horseshoe.

He popped up between the piles on his desk and said irritably, 'Well sit down, Angel. There. Opposite me. Where I can see you. That's it.'

Angel sat down on the only chair his side of the desk.

'How are you getting on with this Piggott murder?'

'Not very well. There are no witnesses, no forensics, nothing.'

'SOC not turned up anything?'

'No, sir.'

'If the media get hold of that tip we had from Special Branch, they're going to take us to the cleaners. You should have immediately taken over his personal security and put him in the safe house for a month or so. If that comes out, you know you will be disciplined.'

Angel's pulse raced. His lips tightened. 'There were a hundred reasons why I didn't do that,' he said. 'The most significant was that Piggott was unwilling to take the threat seriously. I told you that at the time.'

'I was against it, and I told you *that* at the time.'

'Well, I was against it too, sir, but as Piggott wouldn't cooperate, it was impossible to do anything. Anyway, I remember you saying how expensive it was to keep anybody in the safe house.'

'So it is, but there are occasions when we must use it.'

'We could only have kept Piggott there by force. He wouldn't have stayed there voluntarily.'

'Well, keep onto it. How are you getting on with that film star murder threat? Is the husband Persimmon still in Ireland?'

'Not sure, sir. He could have returned by now. I've heard nothing. And I've been fully taken up with this Piggott case.'

'Has she not taken advantage of his absence to disappear?'

Angel shook his head and rubbed his chin.

Harker smiled. It was a rare occasion. Angel reckoned that every time Superintendent Harker smiled a donkey died.

Then Harker said, 'No one in their right mind is going to tell a police detective he is going to murder his wife — and then go ahead and do it.'

* * *

The next day, the day of Cecil Piggott's funeral, DS Carter drove the unmarked car taking DI Angel to St Peter's Church in the town centre of Bromersley. She stopped outside the black iron gates.

They saw the police observation van painted up with the words 'Walker's Removals' appropriately parked outside the church gates.

Angel nodded approvingly. 'Crisp has certainly got himself a plum position.'

'It'll be good, sir,' she said.

'I hope so. This is the only chance of us getting a suspect,' he said as he got out of the car. 'I hope I don't look like a copper.'

'You look as if you're straight out of a posh tailor's window,' she said. 'Going to the Lord Mayor's funeral.'

He smiled. 'I hope that's a compliment,' he said as he closed the car door.

Flora laughed as she drove away.

Angel made his way through the gateway, along the drive towards the church door. Out of the corner of his eye he couldn't help noticing a pile of earth and a hole in the ground big enough to receive a coffin.

He wrinkled his nose and sighed as he briefly imagined it was for his own coffin, or worse, for Mary's.

He removed his hat and stepped through the porch and into the church.

There were very few people around.

An usher in a worn-out black cloak gave him a prayer book, and with a gesture of his arm invited him to sit somewhere towards the front of the church.

Angel looked round at the twenty or so mostly elderly people seated haphazardly in groups of two or three towards the front and in the pews at the end of the centre aisle. They looked lost in the vastness of the building.

He elected to sit on the end of a row at the far side several rows from the back, so that he could observe everybody in the congregation.

He checked his watch. It was 10.58 a.m.

Then he looked up and saw two bulky men in camelhair coats come in. The bigger one — who, judging by the size and structure of his mouth, would win no beauty contests — surreptitiously said something to the other, who nodded, walked to the front of the church and sat on the end of the front row. The big man sat on a pew at the back, nearest the entrance.

Angel pursed his lips. He wasn't pleased. He didn't know the two men, but in his experience they looked like trouble.

He needed to make a phone call to DS Flora Carter. And quick.

He checked his watch again. It was 10.59 a.m.

A young man with tousled hair and a crumpled suit rushed in. He was given a prayer book and he took a pew on the front row with Mrs Piggott and the other woman. The two women smiled, held out their hands and made room for him to sit between them. He smiled back and gave them both a dutiful kiss.

Angel recognised him. It was the deceased's teara-way son, Arthur Piggott. He was wanted for vehicle theft, breaking and entering, assault and several other smaller offences.

Angel tightened his jaw muscles. It was an awful time to collar a man, but Piggott was a nuisance to society and had never done an honest day's work in his life. Angel was determined to arrest him at the first opportunity.

The organ began to play and the usher promptly opened the double doors of the church.

The congregation rose to its feet.

A few moments later, a priest led the small procession of coffin bearers and the funeral director into the church. As they reached the aisle, the priest began to intone the words, 'I am the resurrection and the life, saith the Lord: he that believeth in me . . .'

Angel quietly left his pew, crossed the back of the church and slipped between the big doors as the usher was closing them. The usher let him pass, but screwed up his face and shook his head in disapproval.

Outside in the porch was a tall, lean man talking on his mobile, his back to Angel. He was wearing a smart, light-coloured suit, and brown-and-white leather shoes, pretty conspicuous in this day and age and for such an occasion. He turned to see Angel then quickly turned away and put the phone closer to his mouth.

Angel likewise didn't want to be overheard. He stepped smartly through the porch and out into the church drive. He took out his mobile and selected DS Carter's number. It rang out.

'Flora,' he said, 'two heavies have turned up. There may be more. And young Piggott's arrived. I want some backup

44

here ASAP. Preferably in plain clothes. These gorillas could be armed. I need at least eight men.'

'Do you want me to phone Wakefield for the armed unit, sir?'

'There isn't time. Hurry up. They've got to be here in about six minutes!'

The line went momentarily silent.

'Do my best, sir,' she said.

Then Angel called DS Crisp, who was only yards away in the detection van with Cadet Cassandra Jagger.

'I want you out here, Crisp. Let Cassandra do the Cecil B. DeMille bit.'

* * *

The small congregation followed the coffin outside and gathered round the grave with the neat pile of moist earth alongside it.

Angel looked around the gate area beyond the detection van for signs of police vehicles and reinforcements but could see nothing.

His fists tightened as he sighed and quietly joined the mourners.

The priest began saying prayers for the interment as the bearers lowered the coffin into the grave, and on the words 'ashes to ashes, dust to dust', one of them sprinkled a handful of earth over the grave. It rattled and echoed as it hit the coffin lid.

Angel saw that the two heavies had worked their way into positions immediately behind the widow, Mrs Piggott. Angel managed to get behind the bigger of the two men, while with a jerk of the head he directed Crisp to close in to the other.

The priest ended the burial service with a blessing, closed his book, shook hands with Mrs Piggott and offered a few kind words. She thanked him and he made his way back to the church.

The mourners slowly made their way up the drive to their cars.

Mrs Piggott and her son took a last look down at the grave and then briefly put their arms out and hugged each other.

The funeral director came up to them, pointed to the limousine on the drive and said, 'The car is there for you, Mrs Piggott, when you are ready.'

At this point, the bigger of the two heavies stepped forward, leaned over to Mrs Piggott's son, grabbed him by the wrist and pulled his arm up his back.

'The boss wants to see you, son,' the heavy said. 'You're coming with me.'

Arthur Piggott squealed. 'That hurts! Who the hell are you?'

Mrs Piggott shrieked, 'Let him go!'

From behind him, Angel stepped forward. 'Police! Release him!'

With his free hand, the heavy made a fist and thrust it into Angel's face.

Angel was expecting it and it made only a glancing blow, doing little damage.

The other heavy had drawn back his arm to deliver a punch at Angel, when Crisp joined the fray and threw a fist, which landed on his chin and took him by surprise. Thereafter, the man turned his attentions to Crisp, who energetically retaliated.

At the same time, Angel let go two jabs to the bigger man's chin and cheek, and the man released his grip on Arthur Piggott.

His mother grabbed hold of her son and the two of them rushed off to the limousine. The funeral director was waiting to help them inside, then drove off quickly.

Angel was managing the fight well and added a blow to the man's ample stomach in an effort to see where he was most vulnerable. The man grunted in pain and bent forward, and Angel brought up his knee and caught him in the face.

The man grabbed Angel by the lapels on his jacket and pushed him against the cemetery wall, banging his head again and again. But Angel brought his hands up and battered him hard on his ears with clenched fists until he released him. Angel looked round for a weapon. He found a shovel. Bracing the shovel's handle with both hands, Angel drove it into the man's stomach and then delivered a clean sweep to the back of his legs, causing the huge man to stagger backwards, trip over a plank supporting the graveside, and lose his balance. With a loud clatter, he fell into the open grave and onto the coffin lid.

At the same time Crisp took a mighty blow on the chin himself from the lighter of the two heavies, which sent him reeling across the church drive. The big man followed through, kicking Crisp in the head, stomach, everywhere . . .

Angel saw this. The muscles in his face tightened. He left his man in the grave momentarily to give the man kicking Crisp a blow to his head with the shovel, knocking him to the ground.

It gave Crisp the opportunity to get back to his feet.

Angel stood there, breathing heavily, with beads of perspiration on his forehead. He wiped his hair out of his eyes and looked back to see the bigger heavy struggling to climb out of the grave, then he glanced up to the gate to see if any backup had arrived. There was still no sign. However, there was a group of sightseers — maybe as many as fifty — gathering round the gate.

There was the sound of a cry followed by a groan.

Angel turned back to see Crisp in a heap on the drive with a stone at the side of him, and the heavy running up the drive into the small crowd.

Angel rushed across to Crisp and saw blood running from his temple. He lifted his head into his lap and attempted to stop the flow with his handkerchief.

Then he saw DS Flora Carter running down the drive towards him followed by DC Edward Scrivens and several PCs in plain clothes.

'You all right, sir?' Flora said. 'What's happened to Trevor? He looks in a bad way.'

'Get an ambulance,' he said.

Flora took out her mobile and began tapping 999.

Angel then turned back to see how the heavy in the grave was doing. There was nothing to be seen above ground.

Scrivens arrived.

'Look in that grave, Ted. Tell me what you see.'

Scrivens hesitated.

'Hurry up, lad,' Angel said. 'You're not here to model that suit.'

Scrivens picked his way through the earth, round the shovel and peered down into the grave.

Angel's knuckles tightened. 'Is there anybody in there?'

Scrivens frowned. 'There's a coffin partly covered in muck, sir.'

'Nothing else?'

'Well, sir. I suppose there's a body inside the coffin.'

Exasperated, Angel shouted, 'Is there a *live* body down there?'

'I wouldn't know, sir. Not without opening—'

Angel shook his head. 'Never mind,' he said. He wasn't pleased. Obviously, the other heavy had also escaped while he was attending to Crisp.

'Scrivens,' Angel said, 'come here. Hold Crisp's head in your lap like I'm doing. If he comes round, talk to him, and keep him talking.'

When Scrivens took over, Angel stood up and looked round for a car.

DS Carter came back and said, 'Ambulance is on its way. What about you, sir? You'd better go to the hospital and let them check you over.'

'No,' he said. 'Listen up, Flora, get as many cars as you can looking for two big men, a bit dishevelled and maybe in need of some medical attention themselves. See if anybody in the crowd there knows where they went or what transport they used. Somebody may have their registration number. See what you can find out before they all go away and are lost forever. And I urgently need your car. And somebody had better see if that cadet is all right. She's been in that van on her own throughout this dust-up.'

Flora pulled her car keys out of her pocket and passed them over to him.

'Ta. Find those two gangsters. Top of your list,' he said as he rushed off.

FIVE

Angel stopped the unmarked car outside Piggott's scrapyard on Doncaster Road. He got out and walked down the side road beside the high wall at the back of the house. He knocked urgently on the front door then rushed round to the back, just in time to see Arthur Piggott coming out of the house, closing the back door quietly. He was carrying a valise.

Angel said, 'Just the man I was looking for.'

Arthur Piggott stared at him with eyes as big as traffic lights.

Angel snapped one side of a pair of handcuffs on Arthur Piggott's wrist.

'Oh no,' the young man said. 'What's this for?'

'Well, it's not for getting all your sums right, Arthur.' Angel grabbed the other wrist and snapped the remaining cuff onto it. 'There's a list of offences you're wanted for. You're in great demand. But for now, I am arresting you on suspicion of three offences of taking away a motor vehicle without the owner's consent. You do not have to say anything but it may harm your defence if you do not mention, when questioned, something that you later rely on in court. Anything you do say may be used in evidence.'

'But I haven't done nothing.'

'Well, you can tell that to the judge.' Angel quickly patted Piggott down.

Suddenly the door was snatched open and Mrs Piggott appeared in the doorway. She was still in a black overcoat and hat. Her face was scarlet. Her eyes flashed fiercely from the policeman to her son and back.

'What's happening?' she said, then she saw her son's handcuffed wrists. 'Are you arresting him?'

Piggott looked at his mother. 'It's not right. I haven't done nothing wrong.'

'He hasn't done nothing wrong,' Mrs Piggott echoed.

Angel said, 'Then he has nothing to worry about.'

'Well, what are you arresting him for?'

'Because there are witnesses who say otherwise, Mrs Piggott,' Angel said.

'They're liars,' Piggott said. 'All of them.'

Mrs Piggott said, 'There are people who are against hard-working honest folk like us.'

'Get your son a solicitor, Mrs Piggott. That's the best thing you can do for him.'

'Oh dear,' she said, putting a hand to her forehead.

Angel realised what an absolutely awful day it had been for her. 'You can visit him while he's at the station, Mrs Piggott.'

Then Angel, holding the chain on the handcuffs, tugged it and said, 'Come on, Arthur. You've had a good run for your money,' and led him towards his car.

Mrs Piggott stood on the doorstep, dabbing her eyes with a tissue until the car was out of sight.

***

It had been a long day and it was turning dark when Angel drove the BMW into his garage on Park Street on the Forest Hill estate. He pulled down the up-and-over garage door, locked it and turned to go along the path to the back door of his bungalow, when he heard the front door open and his wife Mary call out.

'Are you all right? Have you seen the time?'

'Yes, yes,' he said. 'I know. I know. I'm coming. You go in, love. It's turning cold.'

He stepped into the hall and blinked when his face hit the light.

She looked up at him.

He couldn't hide the bruising and redness on his face.

Her jaw dropped open. 'Oh, Michael! Whatever have you done to your face? Oh, darling . . . I shall have to bathe that.' She looked at the rest of him. 'And your best suit. It's ruined. What's this? Mud. Whatever have you been doing? Are you hurt anywhere else?'

'No,' he said, and they kissed gently.

'You sure? Oh, Michael, whatever's happened?'

He shrugged and deliberately licked his lips. 'I'm starving. Isn't there any food in this establishment?'

Mary looked at him seriously. 'Michael Angel, you can't just change the subject.'

Angel grinned. 'Why not? It's worked before.'

'Well, it won't work this time,' she said with her arms akimbo.

'Erm, well . . . Trevor Crisp and I became involved in a punch-up — one we didn't instigate. That's all there is to it.'

'Trevor Crisp as well? And how is he?'

'I'm going to phone the hospital later to find out.'

'*Hospital?* He's in hospital? Oh, Michael. It could have been *you*.' She kissed him again. 'Why don't you get a proper job, a safe job . . . a teacher, or something at the town hall, or we could open a shop.'

Angel moaned. 'Oh, Mary, we're not going through all *that* again, are we?'

'Well, you *would* come home at a regular time. It *wouldn't* be dangerous. And you would never have to take a beating ever again.'

'Mary, it's not dangerous really . . . and it's not often I have to get physical, is it?'

'Well it's too often for my liking. And it *is* dangerous. I've known one or two police widows. One day, your luck will run out.'

'Look, Mary, I love you far too much to allow that to happen. I have as strong a desire to live as anybody.'

'I should hope so. Now, go and get a quick shower, change into your clean pyjamas on the bed, come into the kitchen and I'll see if I can find you something to eat.'

'Some dry crusts of bread and the rind off the cheese, ma'am, if you can spare them,' he said.

She had to smile. 'What? You ungrateful guttersnipe. Certainly not. I have some watered-down gruel for you.'

* * *

The following morning, Angel was in his office with DS Carter sorting through the previous day's events when there was a knock at the door.

Angel looked up. It was DS Crisp. He had a large lint bandage stuck to the side of his head above an ear.

'Are you busy, sir?'

'Come in, lad. How are you feeling?'

DS Carter said, 'Hello, Trevor. Sorry to hear about what happened.'

Angel said, 'Nay, don't be too nice to him. He'll be wanting to come back to work.'

Crisp grinned.

He handed Angel a folded piece of paper. 'The doctor has given me a note for seven days, sir.'

Angel didn't look at it. He tossed it into the IN tray on his desk.

'The two monsters,' Angel said. 'Did you recognise them?'

'No, sir. All I can be sure of is that they were after Arthur Piggott. One of them said his boss wanted him.'

'Aye,' Angel nodded. 'And while you were punching each other did you notice anything peculiar about him, anything that we might be able to use to identify him?'

'No, sir,' Crisp said. 'I can't say that I did.'

Angel rubbed his chin. 'And did you notice a man in a light-brown suit and brown-and-white shoes?'

'No, sir.'

'Okay. Well, lad, you get off home. Let your mother spoil you. And eat up all your greens.'

Crisp frowned, then grinned and closed the door.

Angel turned to Flora. 'Has Cassie finished printing off the stills from yesterday's funeral?'

'Do you want me to find out, sir?'

'Aye. Put a squib up her backside. I don't want her thinking any time will do.'

Flora grinned and made for the door.

Angel's office phone rang. He picked it up. It was Patrick Harrigan of the Dublin police.

'Got some news for you, Michael,' Harrigan said. 'The signal we had on your suspect, Miles Persimmon, weakened and then expired at around four a.m. this morning. That, of course, indicated that he had left the country, probably by plane, at about 3.45 a.m., possibly returning to England.'

'Thank you, Pat. That's valuable information. I'll do the same for you sometime.'

'It's a pleasure, Michael,' Harrigan said. 'May the saints go with you.'

He replaced the phone. He was determined to go up to the farm again that morning to check on Lisa Maria Gooden, and see if he could either get her out of there or make Persimmon afraid of the consequences should anything happen to her.

In the meantime, he had to see what he could get out of young Piggott.

The duty jailer let him into Piggott's cell. The young man was lying on the bed reading a newspaper.

Angel took in a folding chair, opened it, turned it round and sat on it, leaning forward on its backrest. He placed it at the foot of the bed.

'Good morning, Arthur. Got all you want?' Angel said.

Piggott sat up. 'No. I need to be out of here, and I need my solicitor.'

'I'm sure you'll get out of here eventually. And you won't need your solicitor to tell me the identity of the two monsters DS Crisp and I had the displeasure of saving you from yesterday.'

'You mean the two big guys?'

'I mean the two big guys.'

'I've no idea, Mr Angel.'

Angel's face muscles tightened. 'Do you think they had anything to do with your father's murder?'

'I don't know.'

Angel scratched his head. 'I'll run that past you again, Arthur, just in case you didn't quite hear me. I said, do you think they had anything to do with your father's murder?'

'Possibly.'

'Oh, possibly. We're getting a bit closer. That's good. That's progress.'

Angel breathed deeply, then in a much louder tone said, 'I am damned certain that they were involved in your father's murder! Don't you want to put your father's killers away?'

'Of course I do.'

'Well, why were there so many crooks — you included — at your father's funeral? It wasn't so much a funeral as the Annual General Meeting of the Bromersley branch of Crooks Anonymous.'

He was interrupted by a knock on the cell door followed by a rattle of keys.

Angel's face showed he wasn't pleased. He didn't like being interrupted while he was interviewing a suspect.

'What do you want?' he bawled. 'And who is it?'

The cell door opened and DS Flora Carter put her head round it. Her face was like death. 'Something *very* important, sir.' She tilted her head to indicate that she would like him to come out of the cell.

He frowned as he closed the door and glared at her. 'Well, what is it, Flora?'

'I was sure you'd want to know right away — I've just heard on the radio that Lisa Maria Gooden is dead. Died of heart failure a fortnight ago, while her husband was away in Ireland.'

Angel's jaw dropped. He blew out half a lungful of air. Then he turned to Carter and said, 'Why is it that I'm only just hearing about this now?'

She shrugged her shoulders. 'It's only just been announced, sir.'

He shook his head several times then growled, 'You mean it's been deliberately held back by her *beloved* husband.'

* * *

Angel, accompanied by DS Carter, raced up to Persimmon's farm near Tunistone. He turned the BMW through the black wrought-iron gates and followed the lane through the trees, bushes and lawns to the white gravelled area in front of the big farmhouse.

A high-power Italian sports car was parked on the gravel.

Angel glanced at it. While it was a magnificent car, it was greatly incongruous and would be uncomfortably cold in England at that time of the year.

He parked the BMW next to it, and as he was getting out of the car, he saw a young woman of about twenty-five get out of the neighbouring vehicle. She had bleached hair the colour of straw, and was wearing an astrakhan coat and large sunglasses, through which she looked across at him.

Their eyes met.

Angel said a polite 'Good morning.'

The young woman whipped off the sunglasses then flashed her teeth.

'Good morning,' she said, then proceeded to look both Angel and Carter up and down. 'My name's Gloria Griffiths. You aiming to see Miles? He won't see you unless you're invited.'

'Well, erm, thank you. I guess we'll take a chance on that, miss.'

'Good luck,' she said, then started up the sports car. It roared like a lion.

Angel shook his head with disapproval. Carter looked pained.

Gloria Griffiths jabbed at the accelerator pedal several times, roaring the engine again before the car took off.

Angel's attention was diverted away from her by the arrival of the SOC van with DS Taylor and his team. He climbed the stone steps with Carter and she pressed the doorbell.

DS Taylor parked the SOC van behind the BMW and his team began to unload. They were all dressed in white with their heads covered and wearing white gloves.

The door was opened by the young housemaid who was with Mrs Gooden when Angel last called at the house. She recognised Angel immediately. A red flush crept across her cheeks and she began to fidget with the lace on the edge of her apron as she saw the team of officers behind him.

'Oh,' she stammered. 'You'll be wanting to see Mr Persimmon?'

Angel said, 'Yes, please.'

She looked deliberately over the top of Angel's trilby hat and in a stilted delivery said, 'I regret to inform you that . . . er . . . Mr Persimmon is out.'

'Good, that'll make things easier,' Angel said. 'Excuse me, miss,' he said as he stepped into the hall. 'My team and I are here to *search* the house.'

He waved Carter, Taylor and the SOC team to follow his lead.

'You all know what to do,' Angel said as they piled into the hall.

He looked around and noticed a suitcase on the hall table.

'Oh dear,' the maid said.

'Now what the hell is happening, Sarah?' the voice of Miles Persimmon boomed out.

Persimmon walked down the hall towards him. 'What's all this nonsense, Angel?'

'No nonsense, Mr Persimmon,' Angel said, waving a paper at him. 'I have a warrant.'

'Rubbish,' Persimmon said, snatching it from him. 'What for?'

'To search this house and outbuildings.'

Persimmon began to read it.

'I need my solicitor,' he said.

Angel smiled. 'No you don't, sir. Even without any knowledge of the law it is simple to understand. We have the authority of the—'

'All right, all right. Get on with it. You won't find anything illegal in this house.'

'You never know,' Angel said. 'Even a great mind like yours may have forgotten something.'

Persimmon stared at him momentarily, then managed a cynical smile. 'Possible, but highly unlikely.'

'I will need a statement from you about what actually happened. For instance, where did your wife die?'

'I don't actually know. I was in Ireland at the time,' he said, then held a hand out towards the maid. 'Sarah here, Miss Smith, found her. She knows *all* about it.'

Her chin trembled. 'I do, sir.'

Angel looked back at Persimmon. 'And when did you get back from Ireland?'

'I'll leave you with her, Inspector,' he said, pointedly ignoring the question as he walked briskly away down the hall. 'She knows all that has happened.'

Angel called after him, 'Even so, I want a statement from *you*, sir.'

Persimmon was back in his office and closed the door with a bang.

Angel turned to the young maid. 'Miss Smith, when did Mr Persimmon return from Ireland?'

'Some time in the early hours, sir. Call me Sarah. Everybody does. He surprised me when he rang the service bell at six o'clock this morning wanting some coffee.'

She pointed to the suitcase on the hall table.

'There's his case,' she said. 'I've got to unpack that yet.'

'Let my sergeant assist you,' he said, turning to DS Carter.

'Of course, sir,' Flora said. And she took hold of the handle and lifted the case off the table.

Angel left the two young women to it and walked down the hall to Persimmon's office. He raised his hand to knock but changed his mind. He put his hand on the handle, pushed the door open and walked in.

Persimmon was seated at his desk with a pen in his hand reading a document. Without looking up he said, 'It's no good, Angel. I haven't time to speak to you now.'

'That's unfortunate, Mr Persimmon, because it's entirely convenient — nay, imperative — that I speak to you *now*.'

Persimmon glanced up from his reading. He looked as if he had been for a walk in the park and trodden in something unpleasant.

'What makes it so imperative?' he said.

'I am investigating the murder of your wife.'

Persimmon took a sip from the silver flask on his desk. 'My wife wasn't murdered. She died of heart failure. Her death certificate says so.'

Angel slowly shook his head. 'Don't play silly buggers, Persimmon. On the eleventh of November, before you went to Ireland, you told me you intended to murder your wife.'

'Even if I did, you'll never prove it.'

'If needs be, I can have her body exhumed.'

Persimmon smiled. 'My dear Angel, she was cremated.'

Angel felt a lead weight drop in his stomach.

His eyes closed momentarily. He shook his head. *How was this possible?* And why was he always the last person to hear what was happening?

SIX

It took Angel a few seconds to recover from the totally unexpected news that most — if not all — the evidence of the murder of Lisa Maria Gooden had been destroyed in that most thorough and pitiless way. It urged him even more than ever to find a way to bring Persimmon to book.

'We are ready to search this room,' he said. 'I must ask you to leave.'

Persimmon wasn't pleased. He dropped the smile, sniffed and said, 'It won't do you any good, Angel.' Then he stood up and smiled. 'You are investigating the perfect murder.'

'Rubbish,' Angel said. 'There's no such thing.'

Persimmon picked up his briefcase from the floor at the side of the desk and began putting the papers he had been working on into it. He added a bulky wodge of paper loosely fastened by tags and several coloured highlighting pens and closed the lid.

Angel saw what Persimmon was doing and said, 'This is a search, sir, and I only want to do this once. You must leave everything where it is.'

Persimmon's mouth tightened. 'This is nothing of signif-
icance — only paperwork to do with my new film.'

'Leave it there, Persimmon,' Angel said.

Persimmon banged the briefcase angrily on the desk. 'Is
it convenient to retire to my bedroom or are your little men
still scrambling around in there?'

Angel took his mobile out of his pocket and tapped in
a number. It was to DS Taylor, who was somewhere in the
house. 'Mr Persimmon is clearing out of his study, Don.'

'Right, sir. We'll be down there in a few minutes.'

Angel put away his mobile and turned to Persimmon.

'Your bedroom will be free soon,' he said, making for
the door.

'I've told you, Angel, you are wasting your time.'

Angel's heartbeat raced. He yanked open the door, pursed
his lips and turned to face Persimmon. 'I'll do a deal with you.
I won't tell you how to make a film if you don't tell me how
to catch a murderer.'

He stormed out and closed the door.

Persimmon smiled, pleased to see that he had ruffled
Angel's feathers.

* * *

'What's in here?' Angel said, standing with the young maid
at a door upstairs.

Sarah Smith opened it and said, 'This is Miss Gooden's
bedroom.'

Angel looked around the huge room, luxuriously
appointed with a large half-tester bed with pink voile drapes
at the head, a huge TV screen and a wall of mirrors from floor
to ceiling.

'She died in that bed,' she said with a sniff.

'Hmm. Has the bedding been changed since she died?'

'Oh yes, sir. Mr Persimmon told me to launder everything.'

Angel frowned. 'Who found Miss Gooden's body then?'

'I did. Ooh, it was awful. I brought her breakfast in bed at eight o'clock, as usual. I tried to wake her and it was only then I realised she was . . . that she had passed over.'

'And she had not complained of feeling ill or anything during the previous day or night?'

'No, sir. No. She seemed . . . maybe that she had something on her mind? And she said she was very tired. She slept on and off almost all day . . . bless her.'

Angel ambled round the room. 'So, what did you do then?'

'I telephoned Mr Persimmon in Ireland, of course. He told me to phone for a death certificate and then to ring the undertaker and ask him to phone him back in Ireland. And not to be telling anybody about it.'

'What day was it that Miss Gooden died?'

'It'll be two weeks on Friday, sir. The fifteenth.'

Angel raised his eyebrows. 'That's twelve days ago.'

She nodded.

Angel thought carefully how to construct the next question. 'So, when did Mr Persimmon come back for the funeral?'

'He didn't,' she said. 'I was the only one there, plus the priest and the undertaker's men. He said he was too busy to come over. But I understood. The poor man.'

Angel shook his head. This young woman was either a superb actress or as naive as a new-born babe.

'Well, when did Mr Persimmon return from Ireland?'

'I told you, sir. During the night. The first I saw of him was six o'clock this morning.'

Angel had to believe it. It matched exactly what his Irish friend Harrigan had already reported earlier that morning. He moved on.

'Did the Persimmons have a social life?'

Sarah said, 'Oh yes. They liked to entertain, but their guests were always in the film world. Big important names. Like other actors, writers, technical men, other film directors . . .'

'Didn't they have any friends?'

'I don't think you could call the people they mix with friends, sir. Besides, Miss Gooden wasn't much interested in friends . . . only how to keep slim, how to make herself look more beautiful and buying new clothes. And Mr Persimmon is really only interested in making films,' she said. 'Whatever he does is always to do with the film he's working on at the time. He isn't much interested in anything else.'

Angel nodded. He was standing at the head of the bed next to a bedside cabinet. There was a heart-shaped gilt handle on the drawer. Angel leaned over, pulled it open and peered inside. It was empty apart from a jar of hand cream and three rolls of strong mints, one open. He closed the drawer. His curiosity had been roused. He moved round the bed and opened the drawer in that bedside cabinet. It had several packets of very fine nylon tights. He took them out and underneath found another roll of strong mints. He put the tights back and closed the drawer.

Angel meandered thoughtfully round the room for a few moments then suddenly turned back to Sarah and said, 'Where is Miss Gooden's handbag?'

'I put it in here,' she said, pointing to the wardrobe close behind her.

Angel held out his hand. 'Would you pass it to me, please?'

She opened the wardrobe door and reached down inside.

'I knew it would be important,' she said. 'It was on the dressing table. I was going to give it to Mr Persimmon.'

She passed the handbag to Angel, who opened it and tipped the contents onto the bed.

Sarah looked on.

Angel riffled through the contents systematically. There were mostly the usual items you would expect to find in a woman's handbag. He returned the mundane items but held back her mobile phone, a bunch of keys and what seemed to be a small key fob for a car. He left them on the bed, snapped shut the handbag and passed it to Sarah. 'Would you put that back where it was, please, Sarah?'

He picked up the key fob, raising his eyebrows. 'Did Miss Gooden have a car?'

'Not that I know of,' Sarah said. 'Of course, she didn't really need one. I mean there was the big car and the full-time chauffeur at her beck and call . . . and she could have borrowed Mr Persimmon's Porsche or got a taxi.'

'Hmm,' he said. Then he pointed to the key fob. 'That isn't a key for a Porsche. What car is that for then?'

'I've often wondered that myself,' she said. 'I used to see it in her hand. She tried to hide it like a conjuror . . . particularly from Mr Persimmon. Sometimes it would be on her bedside table, sometimes on the dressing table.'

Angel rubbed his chin. 'That's all for now, Sarah. Thank you.'

* * *

Angel found DS Donald Taylor, head of SOC, and two of his team systematically searching Miles Persimmon's bedroom. Angel gave Taylor the key fob and asked him to find out which car it unlocked. Taylor looked at it — only one button. He pressed it. A tiny red light glowed on it momentarily.

'Right, sir,' he said, putting the key fob in his pocket, and returned to searching the room.

Angel then handed the victim's mobile phone to DC Edward Scrivens and directed him to check it out.

He then saw that DS Carter was interviewing the only other full-time member of staff at the farmhouse: Nick Toulson, the chauffeur and handyman. The police photographer was clicking away at the window catches. Everybody was at work. That was fine.

He wandered out of the front door and looked out at the scene.

The farm had over three acres devoted to garden, which included a large grassy expanse with a small area of pines and other evergreens near the front entrance to protect the privacy of the farmhouse from the road. Near the farmyard side was a wall facing south by which there were many plants, from roses and hollyhocks to plants such as monkshood. There were also foxglove, cuckoo pint and deadly nightshade, enough to poison all of Bromersley.

Angel sighed. He turned and walked back to the house. As he reached the door, he saw a car and driver he recognised coming towards him. It was Dr Mac, the local pathologist.

Angel was pleased to see his friend and fellow worker.

'I didn't call you out, Mac,' he said. 'I didn't think cremated bodies were anything in your line.'

Mac smiled. 'I live near here. I was on my way home to lunch. I've seen the death certificate for Lisa Maria Gooden, Michael, and essentially it says that she died of heart failure.'

'What's the likely cause in this instance?' Angel said.

'I couldn't say. Possibly a few deleterious issues working together.'

'Could she have been poisoned?'

'Very possibly. As the kidneys and liver are cremated, we'll never know.'

Angel sighed heavily. He rubbed his chin hard.

Mac could see he was troubled.

'What's the matter, Michael?' he said.

'Looks like Persimmon has got away with murder,' Angel said. 'And there's nothing I can do about it.'

'What do you mean?'

Angel explained the situation to the older man.

Mac thought for long a moment. 'Well, Michael, you've never been beaten yet. If there's a way, I am sure you'll find it.'

* * *

Angel had the weekend to think about Persimmon. Every hour that passed made him that bit angrier with the situation.

On the Monday morning, Angel arrived at his office and was taking off his coat when the phone rang.

It was Harker. 'Angel, come up here *now*,' he said and then slammed the phone down.

Angel pursed his lips, hung up his coat and hat and marched up the corridor. He knocked on the superintendent's door.

'Ah, Angel, come in. Sit down.'

Angel blinked. The hot office reeked of menthol. He sat down.

'Now, what are you doing with this Arthur Piggott character? Why isn't he charged and remanded to Armley or Doncaster or somewhere?'

'Well, you know, sir,' Angel said. I've been busy with—'

'Do you know what it costs this station to bestow full board and provide twenty-four-seven security to these little crooks?' Harker said.

'No, sir. But I'm sure you're going to tell me.'

'About £200 a day. Either get him charged or move on.'

'If I'm not careful he'll disappear back into the underworld, sir. And it will take years to find him again. Also, the murder of his father has not yet been solved and Arthur Piggott might be able to assist us with enquiries.'

'Yes. What are you doing about that?'

'There's no forensic evidence and no witnesses, sir. I have no line of inquiry.'

'Now listen to me. I want you to charge Piggott or release him. I'll give you three more days.'

Angel sighed. 'To do that, sir, I'll have to move my attention away from Miles Persimmon, and he *did* murder his wife. He admitted it.'

'Well, book him then. Don't mess about, lad. Book him. And get *him* off on remand to Armley.'

'The only evidence I have is hearsay. There are no witnesses to prove that he ever told me that he intended killing her.'

'What sort of a character is he? Is he looking for publicity or what?'

'I think it's more publicity than he wants. You must have heard of him, sir. Miles Persimmon.'

He hadn't.

'I would offer to take this Arthur Piggott character off your hands if I wasn't up to my neck,' Harker said.

Angel smiled and shook his head. He had never heard of Harker doing any leg work since he was promoted.

'It's Christmas in three weeks,' Harker said. 'And I'm stuck for a Father Christmas for the children's party. The usual man has retired. It's all very difficult.'

* * *

It was 8.35 a.m. on Tuesday, 3 December.

Angel was in his office dealing with the post when there was knock on the door. It was DS Crisp reporting for duty after his seven days recovering from the injury sustained at Cecil Piggott's funeral.

Angel welcomed him back and immediately passed him the files on Arthur Piggott and his late father. He relayed the attitude of Detective Superintendent Harker towards getting Arthur charged and remanded to make a financial saving of the station's funds.

Crisp was delighted to be given a job on his own and rushed off. His first consideration was to charge the man with anything in the book that could hold him.

DS Taylor knocked on the door and came in. 'Have you a minute, sir?'

'What is it, Don?'

'It's this,' he said, waving the key fob found in Lisa Maria Gooden's handbag.

'Ah yes,' Angel said, his eyebrows raising. 'What have you got?'

'I was told that this is not a remote for a particular make of car, nor is it for a television or radio. It's the sort used in security, to switch something on or off remotely, or to unlock or lock a door or a safe . . . that sort of thing.'

That set Angel thinking. What would a famous film star have needed to be so secretive about? And what did the remote key operate?

Angel snatched his coat and hat off the peg. 'Don, if anybody's looking for me I'm at Persimmon's farm.'

* * *

The maid, Sarah Smith, opened the farmhouse door.

'I need to see Mr Persimmon, Sarah, please.'

'I'm afraid he's not in, Mr Angel,' she said.

Angel looked at her, narrowing his eyes.

'I mean it. It's the truth this time,' she protested.

Angel didn't intend to have any more nonsense. He put one foot onto the hall carpet and said, 'I need to check on something.'

She stepped back to give him room, then she closed the door.

Angel frowned. 'Has Mr Persimmon gone away?'

'He's gone to London, sir.'

Angel's eyes narrowed again as he wondered if he had done a bunk.

Sarah added, 'He's gone on business. He'll be back tonight.'

Angel hoped he would be. He held the key fob up to her eyes and said, 'Remember this?'

She nodded.

'I am going throughout the house with this,' he said. 'In fact, anywhere Miss Gooden might have gone, to see if I can find out what it's for. And I'll start right here.'

He walked round the entrance hall, stood in several places and pressed the button. Nothing happened.

Angel clenched his jaw and sighed loudly.

Sarah Smith smirked. 'Well, I'll leave you to it, Inspector. I've some washing to air.' She took off to the kitchen.

Angel repeated the routine in the other downstairs rooms with no success. He hoped he might have better luck upstairs.

He ventured into Miss Gooden's bedroom, directed the remote systematically across the wall, the dressing table, the wardrobe, the bed . . .

And then it happened.

He heard a click.

His mouth opened. He sucked in air silently. His heart raced.

The sound came from one corner of the head of the bed.

He pointed the remote directly at the spot again, pressed the button and listened . . . nothing. He waited longer . . . still nothing. He pressed the button again and again . . . still silence.

He dropped the fob onto the bed and with both hands began to pull away at the pink voile drapes that decorated the head of the bed so glamorously. He moved the pillows and lifted the voile to show the heavy wooden corner bedpost. It revealed a small hinged wooden door in it, which had been released by the remote. He carefully pulled open the little door with a fingernail to find a space about 10 cm square by 30 cm deep which had been hollowed out. He peered into it. It was empty. He looked again at the empty hiding place in the heavy wooden corner post and rubbed his chin. He closed the little door and it made a decisive click. The hiding place was almost invisible. The colour and the grain of the wood matched perfectly. He pressed the button on the remote. As expected, it clicked and flicked open a millimetre or so.

He wondered what on earth Lisa Maria Gooden had wanted to hide. Perhaps gold or diamonds, or papers of some kind — though the latter would have to be rolled or folded excessively.

He closed the small door again with a click, straightened the pink voile drapes, replaced the pillows and smoothed down the covers.

SEVEN

Angel was at the computer in his office writing up his daily report for Detective Superintendent Harker.

DS Crisp knocked on the door and came in carrying a small cardboard box. He put it on the desk.

Angel's eyebrows shot up.

'The still photographs from the video taken at Cecil Piggott's funeral, sir.'

'Oh yes, thank you,' he said, and turned away from the computer. 'Have you identified them all?'

There were thirty stills, about the size of a postcard, mostly head and shoulders and in colour. The system was to find out the name of each person and write it on the back.

'We've identified twenty-seven of them, sir,' Crisp said, 'relations, neighbours and friends of Mrs Piggott, but we haven't got the names of the two heavies and one other . . . a man who nobody seems to know.'

Angel went through them. There was nothing at all interesting in the identified mourners.

He pulled out the stills of the three unidentified men, handed them to Crisp and said, 'Get SOCO to enlarge them as far as they'll go, then print off, say, twenty copies of each.'

'Right, sir.'

'And I want to see the video.'

'I can set it up in the briefing room in about ten minutes, if you want, sir?'

'Right, lad, do that. I'll be down.'

Crisp rushed off and bumped into Ted Scrivens, who was making his way in to see the inspector.

'Come in, Ted,' Angel said. 'Have you got Cecil Piggott's phone list yet?'

Scrivens waved some papers at Angel. 'That's just what I was coming to see you about, sir.'

'Let's have a look,' Angel said, taking the papers from him. He looked down the list.

Scrivens said, 'They're mostly business calls, sir. They all look innocent enough. Very few personal calls. But there is a number which he seemed to call most days, another mobile. I've dialled it three times — a woman answered, same voice each time. She was as cagey as I was. Wouldn't give her name, wouldn't tell me anything.'

Angel handed the papers back and stood up. 'Right. Find out the phone company and follow it through. And let me know what you get. Must go.'

'Right, sir.'

Angel left the office and headed down the corridor to the briefing room, where the police staff of each shift assembled to receive the orders for the day. There were notices pinned to a large board almost covering one wall, another wall that was all windows and another painted white matt to provide a screen suitable for the projection of film, whether for training or covert observation purposes.

Crisp was at a table in the middle of the room setting up a projector, while Cadet Cassie Jagger was waving a long pole around, pulling down window blinds to darken the room.

Crisp looked up. 'Almost ready, sir.'

Angel took a chair from a pile stacked at one end of the room and sat down.

Cassie finished pulling down the blinds, laid the pole down, took a chair from the stack and sat down.

The video lasted only a few minutes.

'That's it, sir,' Crisp said as white light hit the screen.

At the end Angel said, 'Can you run it back just before the verger opens the church doors?'

'That's where the stranger comes out of the porch and where I was able to pick him up on the camera and take a still,' Crisp said.

'Exactly. Then let's see him a frame at a time. Let's get to know as much of him as we can.' Then Angel turned to the cadet. 'Cassie, will you note what we observe about this character?'

'Right, sir,' she said and took out her notebook.

Crisp soon reached the place.

'That's him, Cassie,' Angel said, his eyes glued to the screen. 'Write this down. He's lean, tanned. Maybe 5' 10". Expensively dressed. Light-brown suit. Brown-and-white leather shoes. Dark brown hair receding only slightly. No specs. No facial hair. Age between forty and sixty-five. Struts about like a Gestapo officer. Face like a car crash—' he rubbed his chin thoughtfully — 'you know, I'm sure I've seen him before.'

Then Angel turned to Crisp. 'Can you add anything, Trevor?'

'He's wearing a black tie, sir.'

Angel pulled a grim face. 'Aye. His only respectful contribution to the memorial of poor old Cecil Piggott's death.'

* * *

DI Angel's office
Bromersley Police Station, South Yorkshire
Thursday, 5 December

All the reports, photographs, interview transcripts and other oddments of information were on Angel's desk, and he was going through them for a chink of light that would hopefully show him how he was to prove that Persimmon had murdered his wife.

Among SOC reports were lists of the contents of the kitchen waste bins as well as the various other waste baskets in the house. Lists of this kind frequently made the most interesting and informative reading. That day was no exception. There was an entry under the kitchen waste bin of empty bottles of brandy, whisky, sherry and several bottles of French wine.

There were other signs of Lisa's extravagance — her dresses, which filled the attic as well as the bedroom, along with two full cases of Belvedere vodka, concealed under a pile of clothes at the back of one of the two wardrobes in the attic where she seemed to stash her mountain of excess clothes.

Angel assumed that the foremost drinker was Persimmon. He probably entertained often and his guests would no doubt drink their share.

Angel rubbed his chin in thought. He read the reports again and again. And the more he thought about it, the more he realised Lisa Maria Gooden was not a recovering alcoholic — despite what she had said.

He returned to the farmhouse and knocked on the door.

It was predictably answered by Sarah Smith, who raised her eyebrows when she saw Angel on the doorstep.

'Good morning, Inspector. I'm afraid Mr Persimmon is out, but he'll be back shortly.'

'Good morning, Sarah,' Angel said. 'It's you I want to see.'

Her lip trembled. 'I've told you all I know, Inspector,' she said.

'Not quite *every*thing, Sarah.'

She froze, no doubt wondering what he knew and what he didn't know.

Eventually, Angel said, 'May I come in?'

'Oh, sorry. Of course.'

She led the way to the sitting room.

'Please sit down,' she said. 'And now, Inspector, what is it?'

'You didn't tell me that Miss Gooden was an alcoholic.'

'But she wasn't. That was years ago. She was over all that.'

Angel shook his head. 'Well, who in the house drinks vodka and needs to have access to strong mints?'

Sarah Smith looked downward. Her brain was working overtime. After a moment or two, she said, 'Well, she was a *recovering* alcoholic, you know?'

'No, she wasn't a *recovering* alcoholic. Not judging by her clandestine supply of vodka. No, Sarah. Lisa Maria Gooden was a fully blown, twenty-four-seven alcoholic, employing all the old tricks to hide her condition from the world.'

Sarah Smith shrugged and sighed. 'Well, if you say so, Mr Angel.'

'And she used to hide the bottle of vodka in a cavity in the leg of her bed.'

Sarah blinked. She didn't know that he had found the hiding place.

'And you could have told me all about it,' Angel continued, 'and saved me some time, instead of wasting public money.'

She looked down at her lap and said nothing.

'You can make up for that if you can tell me if Mr Persimmon knew of the hiding place in her bed?'

'I honestly don't know, Mr Angel. But I know that he knew about her drinking on the sly.'

Angel's eyebrows shot up. 'How do you know that?'

'Because about a year ago, he wanted to see the weekly supermarket bill — he thought it was unreasonably big. He made me bring it to him and go through each entry, and where necessary, explain what it was and what I needed it for and so on. There were four one-litre bottles of Belvedere vodka, and I had to say that they were for Miss Gooden. What else could I say? He asked me if she had started drinking again, and well, I couldn't say no, could I?'

'You said about a year ago?'

'About that.'

Suddenly the front door of the farmhouse opened and closed with a bang and the rattle of a chain.

Sarah jumped up. 'That'll be Mr Persimmon,' she said. 'Excuse me, Mr Angel, I'll have to go.'

She made for the door while brushing down her front with her hand and straightening her apron.

Angel stood up. 'I want to see him,' he called as he followed her.

Sarah reached the hall in time to catch a sweaty Persimmon in a black tracksuit and trainers making for his study.

'Mr Persimmon, I have Inspector Angel in the front sitting room. He's waiting to see you, sir.'

Persimmon growled. 'I haven't time for him.'

Angel heard him as he came into the hall and quickly called out, 'And I can only spare *you* one minute, Mr Persimmon.'

'Do you want coffee for two, sir?' Sarah said.

'No,' Persimmon snapped. 'Make it for *one*,' he called and slammed the study door.

Angel stormed down the hall to Persimmon's study. He threw open the door and charged inside.

Persimmon was standing behind his desk. He glared at Angel. 'I haven't time to play whodunnits, Angel. You'll have to make an appointment. How many times do you want telling? Now for goodness' sake let me get on with my work.'

Angel's face muscles tightened. 'Mr Persimmon, this isn't a game. I now know how you murdered your wife.'

'Bully for you, Sherlock,' Persimmon said. 'And are you going to charge me, handcuff me and march me off to the police station?'

'Not yet,' Angel said.

'Really?' Persimmon said. 'What an unbelievably evil mind you have, Angel. However, the point is, can you prove it?'

'Not yet, but I assure you, it's just a matter of time.'

'Why waste your time, Angel? I told you, you'll never prove a thing against me.'

EIGHT

Angel returned to his car in a trance. He felt a hollowness in his chest. The corners of his mouth were turned down. He was wondering if indeed he ever would be able to prove the man guilty of murder. He began to wonder why he was a policeman at all. Persimmon was always so confident.

He got into the BMW and made for the police station. But his mind wasn't on his driving.

Even though he had discovered *how* Persimmon had murdered his wife, Angel was unable to charge him because he could not prove beyond a shadow of a doubt to an intelligent and upright jury that Persimmon was guilty. A clever barrister might be able to convince them he was innocent.

Angel needed credible witnesses or indisputable criminal pathology to succeed in this case and he had neither.

He arrived back in his office and was soon interrupted by a knock on the door.

It was Trevor Crisp.

'Excuse me, sir. Regarding Cecil Piggott's mobile phone calls, I've heard from the phone company and that number we couldn't identify — it belongs to a Mr Ching of Roscommon Road. Not known to us. No form. But still unusual.'

Angel nodded. 'Let's go and see him then, shall we? Come on.'

They took Angel's BMW.

It was a big stone-built detached house in one of the more affluent parts of Bromersley.

Crisp pressed the doorbell. Nearby was a brightly polished brass plate. It read *Red Lotus Leisure Ltd*. Underneath it, in smaller letters, *Regd. Office*.

Angel pointed in the general direction of the brass plate. 'Ever heard of them?'

Crisp said, 'No, sir.'

The door was answered by a young man in a smart suit, collar and tie.

Angel flashed his ID and badge. 'DI Angel and DS Crisp. We'd like to see Mr Ching, please.'

The young man nodded. 'I see. Excuse me please.' He closed the door.

Angel exchanged glances with Crisp and nodded confidently. Then he tried to remove a non-existent hair from the collar of his overcoat. He gave up as the front door reopened.

The young man nodded again. 'Please, Mr Ching is delighted to meet you. Follow me.'

They passed through a hallway into a lavish sitting room. There were seven or eight chairs in the room, upholstered with linen of the finest quality. Angel couldn't help but admire the elaborate willow-patterned design of the blue-and-white fabric. There was another door from the room leading to the rest of the house.

'Please be seated,' the young man said. 'Mr Ching will be with you shortly.'

He walked out, and moments later, two huge men entered, positioned themselves at each side of the door and folded their arms. Then a thin, bald old man appeared in the doorway.

Angel immediately stood up, and Crisp copied him a second later.

He had a thin white beard and wore a crisp woollen suit with an expensive cut.

'Good morning, gentlemen,' he said as he stepped across the room to take a seat. 'Please sit down. Would you care for some tea?'

'That's very kind, but no thank you,' Angel answered for Crisp as well as himself.

'You are from the police? What can I do for you?'

'We are making investigations into the murder of a gentleman, Mr Cecil Piggott. He was a scrap dealer on Doncaster Road. Was he known to you, Mr Ching?'

'Murder? Well now, Inspector, that's not a nice thing. Not a nice thing at all. I should think his family would be most upset at such news. But why would you come to me, Inspector? How could you possibly make a connection between the unfortunate murdered gentleman and me?'

Angel noticed that although the man's expression remained cool, something fired behind his eyes. Mr Ching was clearly used to having everything his own way. In the boardroom and in life.

'We have to check everything, you know, Mr Ching,' Angel said. 'And in the course of our investigations, we uncovered a trail back here to this phone number.'

Ching frowned. 'I do not understand.'

Angel said, 'Who lives here besides yourself?'

Ching stared at him, silent and expressionless.

Angel's eyebrows knitted together. 'I assume you don't live here on your own, Mr Ching?'

Suddenly Ching stood up, nodded to his men and said, 'Thank you very much.'

'Excuse me, Mr Ching,' Angel said. 'But we have only just started.'

Ching strode purposefully towards the doorway.

Angel and Crisp stood up promptly and exchanged puzzled glances.

'I have more questions I need to ask you, Mr Ching.'

Ching ignored him. He stepped between the two giant bodyguards, exiting the room. The guards turned and followed in his wake.

The young man in the dark suit came in from the other door and said, 'This way, if you please.'

Angel said, 'Mr Ching may not want to answer our questions, but they do have to be answered. Perhaps you could tell me how I might interview whoever else lives here?'

The young man blinked and looked at them while he assembled what he wanted to say. 'It is for Mr Ching to tell you, sir. I don't live here. I know nothing.'

'Can you give a message to Mr Ching?'

'I don't know.'

Angel wasn't pleased. 'What do you mean, you don't know? This is not a game. I am investigating a murder case. I need answers and I need them quickly. If I do not get sensible responses to proper and necessary questions then Mr Ching will be summonsed for obstructing the law. Tell him that. We will wait for his reply.'

The young man nodded curtly and left them.

Crisp and Angel were alone in the hallway.

Suddenly there was the rattle of a letterbox flap in the front door behind them and a letter fluttered to the floor.

They exchanged glances. Angel bent down, picked it up, glanced at the address on the front and put it in his pocket.

After a few moments, the heavies returned and stood either side of the door to the remainder of house.

Crisp came up to Angel and quietly said, 'What are we going to do if Ching decides he won't be interviewed, sir?'

'What we always do. Follow it through. We'll bring him in to the station if we have to.'

'I know, sir. But I don't fancy taking on either of these two,' Crisp said, casting a meaningful glance at the body-guards' huge biceps.

The young man in the dark lounge suit came back through the doorway. 'Mr Ching will see you again now. Please come this way.'

He led them back into the sitting room and invited them to sit down in the same chairs as before. Shortly, Mr Ching arrived and took a chair facing them.

He tried to smile, which appeared difficult for him, then said, 'Inspector and Sergeant, I regret that our discussions ended so abruptly. It came about because you asked me who lives here. My granddaughters do. I would do anything to keep them out of something so sordid as dealing with the police.'

'Mr Ching,' Angel said, 'it's natural to want to protect your family. But of course, you, like everyone else, are expected to comply with the laws of the land.'

Ching bowed his head in agreement.

Angel continued, 'Simply, what I want to ask you about is this: A man, a family man, Cecil Piggott, was murdered on his own premises. He was not a wicked man, but tragically he is dead, and his wife and family are grief-stricken. In murder cases, we always check the victim's mobile phone to find out as much as we can about them. We have made about twenty other inquiries of calls made by Mr Piggott. Among our inquiries we noted that he frequently made phone calls to your phone. I have the dates and the times. I even have the length of the calls. Now the calls may well be perfectly innocent. All I need is the person Mr Piggott spoke to, and the essence of their conversation, that's all.'

Ching smiled. 'Ah, there is light throughout the tunnel, Inspector Angel. I foresee no difficulty whatsoever in settling this matter. There are certain steps I must take first.'

A mobile phone rang out.

Angel looked at Ching. Then at Crisp.

Ching looked at each of the policemen in turn.

Then Angel said, 'It's mine.'

He dived into his inside pocket and pulled out his mobile. The screen showed him that the caller was Detective Superintendent Harker.

He looked at Ching. 'Excuse me, Mr Ching. I have to take this call. It's my boss.'

Ching nodded. 'You must always listen to your superiors.'

'Is that Angel? Where are you?' Harker bawled. He sounded angry. 'Never mind. An important development has arisen here. I must see you straightaway.'

'Can it wait a few minutes, sir?' Angel said. 'I am at a critical point with—'

'*No it cannot!*' Harker bellowed. 'This is *extremely* urgent.'

Angel wondered what on earth could have happened. Surely Persimmon hadn't given himself up.

'On my way, sir,' he said.

He closed the phone and looked across at Ching.

'Please excuse me, Mr Ching. That was my superintendent. I have been ordered back to the station. I *have* to go. I will get back to you as soon as I can.'

'Very well, Inspector Angel.'

When they were in the car Angel turned to Crisp and said, 'Do you know, I think Ching was relieved at us being called away. Strange man.'

'A very strange man,' Crisp echoed. 'I wonder if we can trust him?'

'I wish we'd had more time to find out. But when the boss yells for you, you obey him. The super wants me, I come running . . . I wonder what's happened.'

'Not another murder, sir?'

Angel's mouth fell open. 'I hope not.'

* * *

Angel knocked on the door to Superintendent Horace Harker's office and walked in, ignoring the heat and smell of menthol. He was used to it.

The big man was seated at his desk reading a letter. He looked up, threw down the letter and said, 'Come in. Sit down. How is it that when I want you, you're never in your office?'

'I was out making inquiries, sir.'

'You're always making inquiries. Were you making inquiries about Arthur Piggott?'

'Indirectly. I was actually making inquiries about the murder of his father.'

'Do you realise we've been providing bed and room service as well as security to Arthur Piggott for the past nine nights? He's being better treated here than he would be if he was living at Claridge's. And three days ago, I gave you three days to get him out of our cells here and onto remand or released.'

Angel wrinkled his nose. 'It's a question of priorities, sir. Isn't it better to try and pick up evidence in a murder case while it is fresh rather than be more concerned about a man safely in custody on much less serious charges?'

Harker's face turned scarlet. 'Are you arguing with me? Let me remind you I was a copper when you were still in nappies. I am running this station and I have given you a direct instruction. It's a matter of balancing costs in relation to results. Either bring a charge against young Piggott enough to get him remanded or I will let him go free.'

Angel came out of Harker's office and slammed the door. He kicked an imaginary empty cigarette packet down the corridor with all the energy he could muster.

He put his head in the detectives' room looking for Crisp. He saw him at his desk tapping at his computer. Crisp saw him coming and stood up.

'You want me, sir?'

'How far have you got to charging Arthur Piggott?'

'I did some digging and have since charged Piggott with stealing a car four years ago, as that seemed to be the quickest, easiest thing to prove.'

'Good. That will be enough to hold him.'

'And I was just tapping out details of the car. There were two witnesses. I've found the statements they gave to Ted Scrivens at the time.'

Angel's eyebrows shot up. 'Grab hold of Scrivens and tell him from me that he is to assist you and to give this job priority. He can check on the owner and those two witnesses. I hope they are all still alive, healthy and sober.'

'Right, sir.'

Angel frowned. 'Something else,' he said. He half-closed his eyes and rubbed his forehead. 'Oh, yes, phone the Fraud office and ask them if they have anything on Red Lotus Leisure Limited. Find out whatever you can.'

Angel made his way across to his office and took out the envelope he had purloined at Ching's. He noted that it was addressed to Red Lotus Leisure. Using a sharp letter opener, he slit the envelope open at the top and took out the A4 sheet of paper. *Is this what it's come to, Angel?* He sighed as he turned the paper over in his hands. He wasn't exactly proud of his methods, but Ching had left him no option.

It was a statement of account from an electrician in Bradford for work done for Red Lotus Leisure. Angel glanced down the list.

28.10.19	at Restaurant, Hope Street, Bromersley
	— £220.00
29.10.19	at Kit Kat Night Club, Front Street, Bradford
	— £480.00
31.10.19	at Restaurant, Dove Cliff Road, Rotherham
	— £224.40
1.11.19	at Billiard Hall, Oak Avenue, Parkgate
	— £409.00
4.11.19	at Takeaway, Sefton Street, Wombwell
	— £260.00
7.11.19	at 113 Skipton Street, Bradford
	— £410.00

Total — £2003.40

Angel took the statement to his computer, connected it to the scanner and made a copy of it. He folded the copy and put it in his inside pocket. The original he put back in the envelope it came in, sealed it across the top with a narrow strip of Sellotape and dropped it in the mailbox at reception.

NINE

Angel was glad to clock out that day.

At home, after supper, he stood up and gave Mary a kiss. The spontaneity surprised her.

'What's that for?' she said with a smile.

'That's for being such a good cook,' he said, and then he kissed her again, taking three times as long.

'And what's *that* for?'

'That's for everything else.'

She smiled.

He retired into the sitting room, and she followed him through a few minutes later carrying two cups of coffee. She found him sat in his favourite chair staring straight ahead and rubbing his chin. She put the cups down on the library table and sat down beside him.

'What's the matter?' she said.

He sighed. 'This case. It's driving me mad.'

He reached out for the cup.

'Michael Angel, your work starts at 8.30 in the morning and finishes at 5.30 at night. It is now almost seven o'clock. Leave it alone until the morning.'

'I wish I could, Mary darling, I really do. I have a situation where a man has privately admitted to me that he has murdered his wife. Furthermore, I now know *how* he did it. But can I *hell* as prove it!'

She put her hand on his. 'Maybe there just *isn't* a way.'

'That's another thing,' he said. 'He is so damned confident that I won't be able to. But there *is* a way. There *must* be a way.'

'Well you know all the details of the case, all the fine points of the law. If there is a way, you'll find it. I know you will. But you should rest now. Give yourself a holiday from it.'

He ran his hand through his hair. 'I've tried it, darling,' he said. 'But I always come back to it.'

Mary took a sip of her coffee.

'Do you know, sweetheart,' she said, 'I read somewhere that if you have a problem . . . like this one seems to be . . . if you feed your mind with all the details of it, your brain will continue subconsciously working on it even when you have consciously stopped thinking about it. And then, if there is an answer, when you least expect it, out pops the solution. Things like that have happened to me, so I know it's right.'

Angel looked at her and smiled. 'Yes. It's happened to me too.'

'Well now, there's a good film on tonight,' she said, pointing at the television.

* * *

It was the early hours of the following morning, Friday, 6 December.

In the foggy blackness of the night, Angel stirred. One moment he was fast asleep in bed with an arm around Mary, the next he was wide awake and as bright as the north star.

He gently disentangled himself from around Mary's shoulder, rolled over and looked upwards at the bedroom ceiling.

His mind raced to the burning question of how to prove Miles Persimmon had murdered his wife, Lisa Maria Gooden. And he suddenly realised he had the solution. That's what must have woken him up.

Angel recalled that Persimmon had been married before and that his first wife had also died young. Her death certificate stated that she had died of heart failure and that she was buried in Bromersley cemetery. Angel therefore reasoned that if Persimmon's first wife had been poisoned and her death certificate read heart failure, then it would be a reasonable assumption (in this particular case) that if his second wife's death certificate read heart failure then she had also possibly been poisoned. If that was checked and proved to be the case, he would then be able to charge Persimmon with two murders!

Angel was elated.

He couldn't get to his office quickly enough. It would require an exhumation order of Persimmon's first wife.

He must get up.

He whisked back the duvet.

Angel's eyes glowed with excitement. His pulse raced. He was confident he had got Persimmon this time.

* * *

After he had applied and been granted the exhumation order for Persimmon's first wife and had passed the order to the cemetery manager, he returned to his office.

Waiting for him was DS Don Taylor from SOC. He was holding a plaster cast of a shoe print.

'Got a minute, sir?' Taylor said.

Angel looked at the plaster cast he was holding. 'What you got?'

'It's from Piggott's scrapyard. We picked up a whole trail of them. This is the best example to show the detail.'

Angel took hold of it. 'It's unevenly worn, isn't it?'

'We think it's size seven,' Taylor said. 'There's a whole trail of them from the gate to Piggott's office.'

Angel frowned. 'Size seven. That's a very small size. This is the left foot. Have you got a right?'

'Crippen had small feet, didn't he, sir?'

Angel frowned. 'I don't know.'

Taylor wished he hadn't mentioned Crippen. 'I believe he did,' he said quickly, then added, 'Yes, we have a right shoe, but it won't be as clean as this.'

'I'd like to see it.'

'I'll sort one out and let you have it, sir.'

Angel pursed his lips. 'Hmm. Can you estimate what time these prints were made?'

'Strangely enough, I *can*, because apart from the suspect's and the victim's, there were no other footprints firm enough for us to take a mould once we'd ruled out Mrs Piggott's and Donohue's. It was early in the day, sir. Say between 06.00 hours and 08.00 hours.'

'Yep, that matches up with what we know. Can you find out anything from the moulding underneath the sole and heel?'

Taylor took back the plaster mould. 'The sole *appears* to be leather. The heel is definitely rubber. There's the maker's brand name . . . looks like Echo, or Elmo, or something like that.'

Angel said, 'Did you find any tyre marks?'

'Yes, sir. Some really excellent examples, but they all turned out to be from Donohue's patrol car, and that was early in the day. There weren't any others from which we could have got a good impression.'

'Right, Don. Keep at it.'

'Yes, sir,' he said and rushed out.

Angel cast a glance at his diary and noticed that for the current day he had written in *11.00. A. Piggott in court.*

He looked at his watch. 10.34 a.m.

He summoned Crisp, who came in wearing his best suit and looking very smart.

Angel said, 'You're in court at eleven. You can manage without me, can't you? Is everything straightforward?'

'Yes, sir. Both witnesses are here. Their evidence sounds good to me. Arthur Piggott is ready for it, and Bloom is representing him.'

Angel wrinkled his nose. He didn't like Mr Bloom. He represented most of the dishonest and unsavoury crooks in the magistrates' court in Bromersley and occasionally had surprising successes.

Angel said, 'All I want to hear is that the case has to be heard in a Crown Court, so he'll be held on remand. That'll keep him shut up for a while. Let me know how it goes.'

Crisp breathed in, pulled in his stomach, stuck out his chest and made himself as tall as he could. 'It'll be all right, sir.'

Angel nodded and Crisp strode out.

Angel leaned back in his chair for a few seconds. He hoped that his wish would be granted. He took out his notebook, turned back a few pages to find a number and tapped it out on his phone.

He went through the usual routine with the woman who answered and was soon put through to Mr Ching.

'Is it convenient for me to call this morning, Mr Ching?' Angel said.

'If you must, Inspector. I thought that you had no need to interview me any further now that you are opening my mail?'

Angel's eyebrows shot up. He didn't think he had been seen.

'I'm not sure I understand what you mean, Mr Ching,' Angel said. 'But perhaps you'd be available to speak to me this morning?'

'I'm not really, Inspector. But to get you off my back, I will make *any* time available.'

'Very well, Mr Ching. I will come straightaway.'

* * *

The atmosphere continued to be icy when he came face to face with Ching.

'Can we make this short, Inspector,' Ching said. 'I am a very busy man, and as you will now know, I have many irons in the fire.'

'I will do my best,' Angel said. 'I was asking why Cecil Piggott made frequent calls to your phone and who he spoke to?'

Ching said, 'I was the one Mr Piggott was addressing on the telephone.'

Angel frowned. It was hard for him to believe. 'Really, Mr Ching?'

'As a scrap metal dealer, Mr Piggott sometimes took in scrap gold. Often old watch cases, wedding rings, broken gold chains and so on. Sometimes he came by gold sovereigns, Krugerrands and even small gold ingots. That's what he would phone about. He would sell the gold to me because I always paid the highest price.'

Angel pursed his lips and rubbed his chin thoughtfully.

Ching said, 'You are wondering why I seem content to pay above the market price?'

'No,' he said. 'You expect the price of gold to rise. I was thinking that when I ring your number, a young female voice answers, and whoever it is, I would like to interview her.'

Angel noticed that Ching's small hands squeezed the chair arms and his face muscles tightened.

'Surely even in the rarefied atmosphere of Bromersley police station you have heard of *receptionists*?' he said.

Angel looked hard at Ching. 'Yes, but they do not serve to shield us from public scrutiny.'

'You want to speak to our receptionist?'

'I'd like to speak in private to anyone in your staff who spoke to Mr Piggott.'

Ching pressed a button on his intercom. 'Yan, the inspector wants to speak to Dawn. Ask her to come down.'

'Yes, Mr Ching,' came the reply.

Ching stood up. 'If you will excuse me. Must get on. My receptionist, Dawn, will be here soon. When you've finished, ask her to tell Yan. He will show you the door. Good day, Inspector.'

Angel nodded and Ching made a quick exit, followed by the two giants.

It was a good five minutes before a woman in her thirties appeared through the door to the rest of the building. She looked across at the policeman.

Angel stood up. 'Dawn? Please come over here and sit down.'

'You must be the inspector.'

'That's right. You're the young woman who usually answers the phone?'

'Yes.'

'Did you speak to Mr Cecil Piggott when he rang?'

'Yes, Inspector. Several times. He asked to speak to Mr Ching.'

'What about?'

'I don't know.'

'You've no idea?'

'Something to do with scrap metal, I suppose,' she said. 'I know that was his business.'

'What else do you know about Mr Piggott, Dawn?'

'He was shot dead. It was in the papers. It was horrible.'

* * *

Daylight was fading fast. Wisps of freezing fog floated in the headlights of the plain black three-ton van used by HMP to transport convicted and remanded prisoners between courts and prisons. The driver and his mate had no idea how unusual the journey that afternoon would prove to be.

On that day, Arthur Piggott was the sole passenger in this specialist vehicle. He was handcuffed, seated, locked and bound in one of the twenty-five individual wire cages.

The case against him had been heard in Bromersley magistrates' court and transferred to the Crown Court, and he was being sent on remand to Pemberley Prison, Astonbury, Sheffield, to await a place and date for his trial.

Astonbury was located off a narrow road through the Dales ten miles long, passing through beautiful scenery on a clear day but very grey that afternoon. The fog continued to descend.

* * *

As the van rumbled its way through the busy streets of Sheffield onto the main road eastwards, a man in a car stolen earlier that afternoon was parked at the side of the road watching the traffic pass.

A black van with the registration number he had been looking for passed him.

He picked up his phone and tapped in a number. 'Hello, Red 5. Red 4 here. Target just checked, heading east.'

'Red 5 to Red 4,' came the reply. 'Got it, Red 4. Out.'

Red 4 pocketed his phone, started the engine and engaged the gear.

He was soon in the country. There was a complete lack of light from houses and streetlights, only black, freezing fog, now hanging in big low clouds.

Red 4 was grateful for the white line. He was relying mostly on that.

His hands were cold so he turned up the heater fan.

He drove the car at 10-mph, sometimes more slowly. There were no vehicles behind him, nor in front, nor coming from the opposite direction. He glanced at his watch. He must be a few minutes behind schedule. It was difficult to judge when he didn't quite know where he was. There was no fog mentioned in the planning of this job. You can't trust the English weather.

Suddenly, ahead of him he saw a red light and then another. It was the HMP van, the target. It was plodding along.

Red 4 had to brake to keep his distance. Then he saw Red 5's lights in his rear-view mirror. He sighed with relief. The plan still looked intact.

They travelled in convoy only a mile or so further when the HMP van suddenly slowed and skidded as the front wheels rolled over 288 broken beer bottles, inevitably followed by the rear wheels. There was the sound of leaking air.

The van came to an abrupt halt.

Then all hell was let loose.

From the side of the road, out of the dark low clouds, three sets of car headlamps suddenly illuminated the HMP van. Five men with white handkerchiefs covering the bottom halves of their faces rushed to it. Two were armed with handguns and three were carrying heavy-duty long-handled cutters.

The driver of the HMP van turned to his co-driver. 'Bugger me! We're under attack, Jack.'

He promptly pressed the red button on his dashboard, which transmitted a pre-recorded message to police stations and prisons that the vehicle was being assaulted. It also triggered a location beacon that would continue transmitting its signal as long as its batteries lasted.

The two armed men rushed to the front of the HMP van waving their handguns. One of them said, 'Put both your hands on the dashboard where we can see them and you won't get hurt.'

At the back, the three men with the heavy-duty cutters had already cut through the hinges and pulled the doors away.

The young man in the cage at the back blinked at them.

'Are you Arthur Piggott?' said one of the men.

'Who are you?'

'We are going to get you out, Arthur. Just be patient.'

They were already in the van cutting through the door of the cage housing Arthur Piggott.

The young man looked confused, surprised, even elated. He couldn't understand why people he didn't know were trying to rescue him.

Meanwhile, Red 4 and Red 5 had both reversed their stolen cars a few metres to leave them sideways, nose to nose, entirely blocking the road to and from Sheffield. Then they had joined one of the getaway cars hidden in the trees just off the road.

A little man rushed up to the back of the HMP van. 'Message from the boss. Hurry up. The bogeys have already received the alarm. They could be here in minutes!'

A voice said, 'Hang on, Titch, and you can take him with you.'

Seconds later they pulled Arthur Piggott from the cage, cut the handcuffs off him, took him to the back of the van and lowered the rather stunned and subdued man to the ground.

The little man said, 'Stick with me, Arthur. Come on.'

Titch ran across the road to a gap in the bushes and Piggott came up behind. Titch pushed Piggott through it and quickly followed him.

At the same time, one of the gang called out, 'Right, everybody! Target achieved. Lights out. Scramble.'

The lights went out. Car doors banged. Exhausts growled in the distance.

Seconds later the site was dark, deserted and as quiet as a grave.

Two minutes after that, a police car siren could be heard in the distance. It very slowly grew louder.

The driver of the HMP van switched on his lights.

* * *

Arthur Piggott was swiftly driven away from the scene by Titch and another man named Crum.

Titch steered the car onto Broad Street in Parkgate. He drove past the front of the Magic Flute, a Chinese restaurant. He took two early turns right and he was at the back door of the restaurant, where a waitress was waiting for them. She let the three of them in and took them into the storeroom, which had a bed, several chairs and a small table with a phone on it.

Titch gave her the keys and she took the car and dumped it in Cheapo's car park in the centre of Rotherham, then transferred to another car she had parked there earlier and drove it back to the rear of the restaurant in Parkgate.

Crum and Titch sat at the table. Piggott slumped onto the bed.

The phone rang. Crum answered it. 'Yeah? . . . Oh yes, boss . . . Got it, boss . . . Right, boss . . . Yes, boss . . . Straightaway, boss.'

He replaced the phone.

'Hey, Arthur,' Crum said. 'You're going to see the boss now. I have to fasten your wrists together and blindfold you.'

Piggott gazed at him for a few seconds. 'What's with this tying up and blindfolding business?'

'Ask the boss when you see him. It's his way. He won't see you if I don't do it.'

Piggott slowly shook his head.

Crum said, 'Please yourself. But as he's the bloke who has just organised and paid for your escape from prison I don't think I'd want to . . . upset him.'

Piggott pursed his lips, then nodded. 'OK,' he said and held out his wrists.

'No,' Crum said. 'He wants you fastened at the back.'

TEN

Crum led the blindfolded man into the car the waitress had exchanged for him and drove for around forty minutes, then guided him out of the car into a building with narrow staircases and many steps.

A piano was being played most beautifully. From the slight echo, Piggott thought the sound was coming from a large empty room or hall. He didn't recognise the tune, but the music was pleasant enough.

Crum knocked on the door.

The piano stopped and a voice called, 'Come in.'

Crum led Arthur into a darkened room. 'I've got Arthur Piggott here, boss.'

'Right, Mr Crum. Well, sit him down somewhere.'

Piggott heard the scrape of a chair on a wooden floor close behind him. Then he was pushed backwards into it.

'That's better. Now me and you can have a little chat. I had a little chat with your father about the money you owed me and he said he would let me have it. But he never showed and then sadly he died. So sad. I don't like it when people die. I don't like going to funerals. Now, Mr Piggott, we don't want anything like that happening to *you*, do we?'

Piggott didn't say anything.

The boss said, 'Pardon?' and waited. Then, 'I said we don't want anything like that happening to *you*, Mr Piggott, do we?'

'No. What is it exactly you're wanting, Mr . . .'

'Ah good. I'm glad you're receiving me. At the last reckoning it was £13,000. With interest for the delay in settling, say £3,000, and this evening's cost of getting you out, say £20,000, I reckon it must be around £36,000. Being a reasonable man, if it is paid in the next couple of days, I'll settle for £35,000.'

Piggott's mouth opened wide. 'Wow! That's a *lot* of money.'

'You're not making the sort of noises I like to hear, Mr Piggott. I think you're forgetting that the day you get this moolah from your ma, pay off this debt, you'll be as free as a bird. The sky will be yours. The sea and the entire earth will be yours. You can start afresh in any part of the world. I've saved you the emptiness, the indignity and the emotions of being held as a criminal awaiting prison. How do you put a value on that? If it was my destiny to receive even a night in prison, I would give almost all I possess to avoid it. And you are looking at *years*. Two years. Five years. Ten years. It goes on. It's your life they're taking from you. I've saved you from all that, and £35,000 is cheap considering what you're getting. I don't think, Mr Piggott, that you fully understand the mathematics of this situation. The costs of running my organisation can be likened to that of running a university. You see, if we use education as our currency — well, education don't come free. I mean, you don't get born with education. Oh no. I mean . . . say your father is an engine driver and your mother is a machinist in a garment factory, when you grow up, you'll be lucky if you get a job washing cars. That's 'cos your father only knows about driving an engine, which you can learn in a few days by watching an experienced driver. His job will be done one day by an automatic mechanical man. And as for your poor old mother, they can do her job out east for a hundredth of what they pay her. Soon automatic machinery will make just about everything. Now then, if you had worked hard and got an education — I mean with letters behind your name, gone to university and had yourself photographed with a cloak and dagger — you'd have more sense than to let yourself wash cars or drive engines or sew up knickers. You can get a thinking job like a barrister, a stockbroker or an accountant. The currency they have to hire out is their education. Their ability to work things out or work their way round things . . . like the law, for instance. Thereafter, the only dirty thing you will ever have to handle is money.'

'I simply haven't got any money.'

'But you can get it. There's the house. There's the scrap metal business, the land, the cash in hand, the stock, the motor vehicles. These are all valuables.'

'It will be my mother's. She's got to live on something. I can't ask her to help me.'

'She loves you, Arthur. You're her son. You came from her. *All* of you came out of her. Think, Arthur, what it's cost me to set up this escape. About eighteen people had a part to play. I had to set up security moves to confuse the fuzz. They're now running up and down the place chasing their own tails. They don't know where to start looking for you.

As long as you're with me you're safe, but I wouldn't fancy your chances if I let you go free. And I might not let you go free. This escape has cost me around £20,000. Seems I have added to my losses. Hmm. Well, it's like this, Mr Piggott: if you have nothing, you speak to your mother and see what she'll give you. You pay me £35,000 in a week or else.'

'It's no use. She'll want whatever there is for herself.'

'If you tell her that your life is at stake . . .'

'*My life?*' he said.

He felt as if a cold rat had run down his spine. His heart raced so fast he thought it might explode.

***

DI Angel's office
Bromersley Police Station, South Yorkshire
Monday, 9 December, 11.05 a.m.

Angel was in his office waiting for news on the examination of the body of Persimmon's first wife.

A lot depended on the pathologist's report, which Dr Mac had said would be known at about 11 a.m. Angel was pacing up and down the tiny office, unable to concentrate on anything except making tentative plans depending on the result.

There was a knock on the door. Angel whipped round to face it.

It was Crisp. He was holding a notebook.

'Dr Mac not rung through yet?' Crisp said.

Angel ran his hand through his hair. 'No. Have you just come in here to annoy me, lad?'

'Oh no, sir. Certainly not. It's just that I've heard from the Fraud office about Red Lotus Leisure, and I thought you'd want to know.'

'What did they say?'

Crisp glanced at his notebook. 'Red Lotus Leisure is not under observation and there are no plans as yet to put the company under observation. It is a private company with fully paid-up capital of £300,000. The directors are Laurence Burton and Shoushan Ching and it was established in 2018.'

'Laurence Burton?' Angel said. 'Who is Laurence Burton?'

'There's nobody with that name on our books. I've checked.'

'Well buzz off and make enquiries. Ask around. See what you can find out about the man. You're a detective, aren't you? Go out and detect.'

Crisp gave Angel a strange look, picked up his notebook and left.

The office phone rang and Angel snatched it up.

'Angel? It's Mac.'

Angel's pulse began to race. He slumped down in the swivel chair. 'What have you got, Mac?' he said.

'You're not going to like it, Michael,' Mac said. 'The woman's liver and kidneys were perfectly healthy, and her heart showed signs of scar tissue and damage to the myocardium that confirmed that the cause of death was heart failure.'

Angel sighed. 'That's that then,' he said.

'Aye. I'm sorry, Michael,' Mac said. 'I wish it could have been otherwise . . .'

'There's no possible chance . . . ?'

'None, Michael. It's confirmed by the coroner. He did the tests. I just witnessed everything.'

'Right, Mac.'

'What are you going to do?'

Angel closed his eyes and shook his head. 'I don't know. Well, thanks, Mac.' He hung up and lowered his head to his chest.

He could hardly believe it. Persimmon had slipped through the net again. He was as slimy and slippery as a school of herring.

Angel was determined to see that Persimmon did not escape justice. He would not allow a man to announce publicly that he intended to murder his wife, then commit the act and get away with it. Oh no.

Angel stood up, reached out for his coat and hat and stalked down the corridor, turning towards the cells and the rear door to the car park. He got into the BMW and drove into the countryside. There was some beautiful scenery around Bromersley. He let the car go further and further into the heart of it, trying to let his mind think of nothing, but found it impossible. After a while, he gave up. He made three left turns then a right, which took him onto a road back to Bromersley. After several miles of green fields and trees he came upon rows of terraced houses, pubs, churches and shops, and then he came to Bromersley cemetery. It was a big expanse of land surrounded by a stone wall topped with metal railings. Inside were hundreds of grey, white, black and natural headstones set on green turf. In the middle of the graves was a two-storey building. Four cars were parked next to it.

He drove in through the entrance and slowly approached the building. He parked the car with the others and looked around at the sea of gravestones.

Suddenly, behind him he heard the sound of an engine. He turned round to see a small bulldozer coming slowly towards him, driven by a man in a blue boiler suit.

Angel stepped to one side.

The man drove the mini digger into a garage in the building and closed the door. Then he walked over to one of the parked cars.

Angel walked across to him.

'Excuse me,' he said, and showed the man his ID and badge. 'Don't suppose you know where Julie Persimmon is buried do you?'

The man smiled. 'I ought to. I've only just filled her back in. She's been up over the week. They brought her back this morning.'

He pointed down the pathway. 'She's along there. Plot number 2601. On the corner. Come on, I'll show you.'

'Thank you,' Angel said.

He set off along the path and Angel joined him.

'I'm the manager here, Inspector,' the man said. 'Walter's my name. I don't get many exhumation orders. Is something funny going on?'

Angel gave Walter a simplified, edited explanation as they strolled along the walkway between the gravestones.

They arrived at Julie Persimmon's grave, and Angel saw the fresh earth that Walter had shovelled back on top of the grave and banged down flat.

Angel strode up onto the turf to read the headstone more clearly. In the process he reached out to the gravestone next to Julie Persimmon's to steady himself and noticed that it was loose. He studied at the bottom of the gravestone where the stone entered the earth and looked behind it.

Scratching his head, he turned to Walter. 'This headstone is loose. It's been moved.'

Walter frowned and pulled some papers out of his pocket. He peered closely at the cemetery plan, then down at the names on the two headstones, then back at the plan, finally looking at Angel in dismay.

'Oh dear! Oh dear!' he said.

'The headstones of the two graves have been switched?'

'Yes.'

'And so the result of the exhumation wasn't that of Julie Persimmon. It was of a woman of similar age who died the year before.'

Walter shook his head but said, 'Yes.'

'And she — like so many people — died of heart failure,' Angel said.

'Apparently.'

Angel smiled thoughtfully. 'So *that's* how he did it,' he muttered.

* * *

It was Tuesday morning, and Angel hadn't wasted any time pursuing a warrant giving the police the authority to exhume the body of Julie Persimmon to permit the necessary medical examination. Furthermore, he was delighted that the arrangements had been made so smoothly. However, he would still have to wait until Thursday for the exhumation and Friday morning before the result of the medical examination could be determined.

He was settled at his desk working through some urgent paperwork when there was a knock at the door.

It was Don Taylor.

'I've brought you the other cast of the sole of the right foot, sir, the one for the probable killer of Cecil Piggott. If you put the pair together you can see that there's a lot of wear on the front right corner of the sole of the right shoe, while the left foot has worn fairly evenly.'

Angel put down his pen and looked at the two plaster casts. 'So he has a limp?'

'A pronounced limp,' Taylor said.

Angel screwed up his eyes in thought. 'You heard from ballistics yet?'

'Yes, sir. Piggott was shot by a .32.'

'Ah. Who do we know that totes a .32 and walks with a limp?'

'I'll get on to Records,' Taylor said.

'Right, Don, and let me know if they come up with any names.'

'Will do, sir,' he said as he stepped out and closed the door.

Angel pursed his lips. He rubbed his chin with the tip of his fingers. Events were moving in his favour for a change. His heart was lighter. Evidence was beginning to come together. He had reckoned he was due for a bit of luck. Surely he had witnessed Persimmon's last trick, and the villain's first wife, Julie, would prove to have been poisoned. He couldn't bear to think where he would go with the case if she had *not* been poisoned.

His thinking was disturbed by another knock on the door.

It was Crisp.

'You wanted me, sir?'

'Yes, Crisp. Drop what you're doing and do a bit of watching and waiting outside Red Lotus Leisure on Roscommon Road. They do more than sell sweet and sour pork and fried rice. In particular I want to know who goes in and who goes out of the place. Take a camera. And binoculars.'

Crisp was pleased. It meant a job out of the station, working from his unmarked car, where he would be more or less his own boss. 'When do you want me to start?'

'An hour ago. You're late.'

Crisp grinned and rushed out.

* * *

DI Angel's office
Bromersley Police Station, South Yorkshire
Friday, 13 December, 8 a.m.

Angel had not had a good night. Today was the day when science would tell Angel whether or not Miles Persimmon's first wife Julie died of poisoning or of heart failure. It had been on his mind what he had to do, whichever way the result went.

He arrived at the police station early that morning. As he took off his coat, he heard the buzzing of that fly that had been annoying him for weeks.

He glanced across his desk looking for a copy of the *Police Gazette*. Eventually he found it in the shallow middle drawer of his desk. He rolled it up and held it tight. Then he looked round the room to try to determine where the buzzing was coming from. When he went to the window, the sound seemed to come from the door, and when he went there the

114

sound seemed to come from the window. Eventually he saw it milling around the light bulb above his head. He gave the fly several mighty swipes, missed it, but caused the light bulb to shake precariously.

He listened. The buzzing had stopped. He waited. He padded quietly around the little office looking for the fly. After a few moments Angel assumed his enemy was resting. He threw down his weapon with relief and sat down.

The phone rang.

His heart missed a beat. He stood up as he reached out for it. 'Angel.'

'Mac here,' said the caller. 'At last you've got the result you needed, Michael. Persimmon's first wife, Julie, died of poisoning, and her heart was in perfect condition.'

Angel felt warm and relieved. 'Thanks, Mac. That is official, isn't it? Nobody can come along and change the facts.'

'Of course not, Michael.'

'Thanks again,' Angel said, and he replaced the phone.

He sat down at his desk. He felt warm. He smiled. He sighed. He opened the middle drawer of his desk and took out the warrants he had prepared earlier, folded them neatly and pushed them into his inside jacket pocket.

Then he jumped up and walked into the hall, across from his office and two doors down, to his opposite number in the uniformed division. It had *Inspector H. Asquith* painted on the door. Angel knocked and pushed it open.

Haydn Asquith was at his desk reading a letter. He looked up.

'Can I come in, Haydn?'

Asquith smiled. 'What's up?'

'I want some uniformed muscle to help me bring in a murderer.'

'Of course, Michael, what do you want?'

'I don't want to put the man on his guard. I want to go quietly. I reckon it will take me about five minutes to get into his house, and *then* I may need your backup. I want your men to block all exits.'

'Leave it with me, Michael. I'll get as many as I can muster.'

'Thanks, Haydn.'

ELEVEN

At noon exactly, two police cars with four constables in each assembled in the compound at the rear of the police station. Ahead of them was Angel, DS Flora Carter, DC Scrivens and PC Weightman in Angel's BMW.

At 12.03 p.m., Angel led the convoy out of the compound and headed as quickly as traffic would allow onto the Manchester Road to Tunistone.

They arrived at Persimmon's farm at 12.18 p.m. and, as arranged, Angel drove his car up the drive and round to the front door, while the two marked police cars waited out of sight of the house at the farm entrance.

Angel got out of the BMW while the others stayed in the car.

It was Sarah Smith who answered the door.

'Good afternoon, Inspector.'

'Good afternoon, Sarah. I want to see Mr Persimmon.'

'I don't think he'll see you. You know what he's like.'

'Where is he, Sarah?'

'In his study, as always. I'll go and ask him.'

'That's all right,' Angel said. 'I'll go down and ask him myself.'

'Oh dear,' she said. 'But, Inspector . . .' She could see trouble was heading her way. She stepped back as Angel pushed the front door further open and the three officers from the car now piled out and followed him down the corridor.

Angel opened the study door and the others followed him in.

Persimmon was seated at his desk. He looked up.

His bottom lip curled angrily. 'What's all this, Angel? What does a man have to do to be allowed to get on with his work without disturbance in his own house?'

The police took up prearranged positions. Angel in front of Persimmon, Weightman behind him, Carter to one side and Scrivens to the other, ready to close in as appropriate.

Angel quickly took the folded sheets of paper out of his pocket. He unfolded them and looked down at the man.

Persimmon stared at each of them in turn.

Angel said, 'Miles Persimmon, I am arresting you for the murders of Julie Persimmon and Lisa Maria Gooden . . .'

'Rubbish. Absolute rubbish,' Persimmon said.

'You do not have to say anything . . .'

Persimmon very slowly opened the right-hand drawer of his desk and reached in.

Standing immediately behind him, Weightman saw him and rammed the drawer shut with his foot trapping Persimmon's wrist.

Persimmon screamed long and loud. It was the sort of scream that a man might make at the moon at midnight on the summer solstice.

Weightman grabbed Persimmon by that wrist and he screamed again.

He checked that Persimmon's hand was empty then he opened the drawer to see what he had been searching for. He pulled out a Beretta Tomcat handgun, a small but very deadly weapon. He checked that the safety catch was on then passed it, butt first, to Carter, who handed it to Angel.

Angel pocketed the gun and referred back to the warrants.

'You do not have to say anything,' Angel read, 'but if you do . . .'

Persimmon suddenly pushed DS Carter out of the way, put up an arm to protect his face and took a running jump at the French windows. There was a heavy bang and the sound of shattered glass as he burst through them and landed on the flagstones outside. Shards of glass were everywhere.

DS Carter and Angel quickly managed to follow him through the damaged windows, and two uniformed PCs outside came running up to him from opposite directions. Persimmon struggled to his feet and tried to run but he had hurt his ankle. The PCs grabbed him, pulled him up and pinned him to the wall of the house.

'Search him and cuff him,' Angel said.

Persimmon screamed obscenities as he fought and struggled and kicked the wall. His face was scarlet, his eyes wide and staring. Panting, he turned his head back as far as he could. He could just see the DI.

'You bastard, Angel,' he said with his mouth overfull with saliva. 'I haven't finished with you yet.'

Angel turned away from him and addressed the others. 'Take him to the nick, put him in a cell but leave the cuffs on until he settles down.'

Four more PCs arrived and assisted with the arrest.

Angel broke away, found a quiet corner, took out his mobile and phoned Sergeant Clifton, who was on duty in the charge room. 'Bernie, Miles Persimmon is on his way down to you.'

'Crikey! You mean the film producer fellow?'

'Yes. Charged with murdering his two wives. You might need assistance. Now, he's to have no visitors. As it leaks out, there's bound to be a lot of press. He can ring his solicitor and obviously his law team are allowed to visit him anytime, but nobody else. But I want to know the names and addresses of those who enquire.'

'Righto, sir.'

* * *

DI Angel's house
Bromersley, South Yorkshire
Saturday, 14 December, 9 a.m.

Angel came back from the bathroom to the bedroom, where Mary was in bed, drinking tea and reading the newspaper. She looked up.

'You've got your suit trousers on, Michael,' she said. 'Are you going out somewhere?'

Before Angel had time to reply, she smiled and said, 'Don't tell me. You're going down to the station to gloat over the new inmate.'

'Not at all,' Angel said, although he did take great delight in having caught Persimmon. 'No, it's just that . . . well, there are some bits and pieces to sort out from yesterday.'

'Well don't get involved in anything that will take a long time, sweetheart. It's your day off, don't forget. It's a day for you to relax. You don't really *have* to show up there until half past eight on Monday.'

'I know. I know,' he said, leaning over the bed and kissing her on her forehead. At the same time, she took his hand and squeezed it.

Twenty minutes later he parked his car at the back of the police station and entered the building by the rear door, which meant passing the cells. He saw the duty jailer and quietly asked him if Persimmon had been a difficult prisoner.

'He was very noisy, swearing and cursing until he spoke to his brief on the station phone, sir. Since then he's settled down. I understand his brief is travelling up from London this morning and should be here at lunchtime.'

'Oh? He didn't want to see Mr Bloom or any other local solicitor?'

'Apparently not, sir. The barrister chap from London is supposed to be a high-flyer.'

'Did you get his name?'

'The sergeant's got it, I'm sure.'

Angel went to seek out Sergeant Clifton.

'How's it going, Bernie?'

'I've just made some tea, sir. Fancy a cup?'

'That would be great,' Angel said. 'Persimmon kept you busy?'

'I should say so. We've had a lot of phone queries from the press. Every newspaper in the world, I should think. About twenty people in the film business. A dozen TV news stations. Half a dozen actors.'

Sergeant Clifton passed Angel a mug of tea and held out an open bag of sugar and a spoon. 'Help yourself, sir.'

Angel brought out one heaped teaspoonful of sugar. 'That'll do it. Thank you, Bernie.' He stirred the tea. 'Any local individuals?'

'No, I don't think so.'

'I hear he hasn't seen his brief yet.'

'He's due sometime today. Persimmon asked to see you several times, by the way. He said it was very important.'

Angel narrowed his eyes. 'I wonder what he wants? I'd better see him, then.'

'And the best of luck, sir,' Clifton said.

Angel smiled, finished the tea and passed the mug across to the duty sergeant.

'Thank you, Bernie,' he said as he waved goodbye.

He approached the duty jailer's desk. The PC stood up.

'Is Persimmon all right, Constable?' Angel said.

'Yes. He keeps asking for you, sir.'

'Aye. That's why I'm here.'

The PC peered through the spy hole. He saw Persimmon lounging on the bed, so he quietly put the key in the lock, turned it and pushed open the door.

'Visitor for you, Persimmon,' the PC said.

'About time,' the prisoner said, getting to his feet. Then he turned, saw it was Angel, looked him up and down and said, 'I suppose you think you can prove the case of murder against me.'

Angel pursed his lips. He licked his bottom lip thoughtfully. 'I haven't time for playing games with you, Persimmon. The fact that you are where you are indicates that we can, doesn't it? Now what did you want to see me about?'

Persimmon wrinkled his nose. 'You can't prove anything, you know. I hope you realise that, Angel. This is your big bluff, isn't it? Well, it isn't going to work.'

'Don't waste any more time, Persimmon. If you just want to bluster and deny the obvious I don't need to be around. And if you won't come to the point, I'm leaving.'

Persimmon's eyes flashed. His tone of voice changed. He came up close to Angel and spoke quickly and quietly.

'Don't go, Inspector. The point is that I have reached the pinnacle of my career. And I am currently working on a screenplay that will rock the world. It is phenomenal. But I need to be out of here, free to develop, produce and direct it. I can't do that in here . . .'

Angel slowly shook his head.

Persimmon continued. 'It is therefore worth it to me to buy my way through any obstruction preventing me from bringing that story to the world. Now, Inspector, you can't *prove* with any certainty that I murdered my wife. *Either* of them.'

Angel began to nod confidently.

Persimmon continued to talk. 'This process will consume a lot of valuable time I can ill afford. To save this time, I am prepared to pay liberally.'

Angel stopped nodding and began shaking his head again.

Persimmon persisted. 'To get me out of this, quickly, secretly and privately, I will give you a quarter of a million pounds. In cash.'

Angel froze. He stopped shaking his head. He stopped moving everything. His mouth fell open.

Over the years, he had been offered bribes of anything up to £10,000 but never as much as £250,000. He was astounded at the amount. It meant that he could pay off the mortgage on the house, his credit card balance, take Mary on a round-the-world cruise and then retire early . . . everything he had ever dreamed of.

'No thank you,' Angel heard himself say.

Persimmon's face went scarlet. 'Did you hear what I said?'

'Absolutely,' Angel said. 'I don't take bribes.'

Persimmon rubbed his chin and screwed up his eyes. 'Half a million, Angel, but that is absolute tops.'

Angel smiled briefly then shook his head. 'I don't believe it,' he said. 'When I say I don't take bribes, I mean *I don't take bribes*.'

Persimmon looked up at the ceiling and opened his hands. He held them out to Angel and said, 'Well, what the hell *do* you want then?'

'*Justice*,' Angel said. 'Justice is enough.'

It clearly wasn't what Persimmon had expected. His eyes flashed in various directions before they landed back on Angel. His thin-lipped, cruel mouth slowly opened. 'You'll pay for this, Angel. By God, you will pay for this. Remember my words.'

Angel had been threatened before. He was used to it. Threats fell off him like beer off a barman's shoe.

* * *

Doncaster Road, Bromersley, South Yorkshire
Sunday, 15 December, 6 p.m.

The sky was as black as fingerprint ink. A streetlamp illuminated part of the pavement three houses from Mrs Piggott's. There were only a few cars and hardly any pedestrians on the move.

A man wearing a thick brown duffle coat and a big old shapeless cap shuffled his way along the quiet road, assisted by a walking stick. He was bent at the waist, the knees and the neck, and took only very small footsteps.

He was not far from Mrs Piggott's house.

A man and a woman holding hands and with arms interlocked walked slowly along the pavement from the opposite direction. They reached the house next door to Mrs Piggott's, stopped, leaned against the gate and immediately fell into an embrace.

A large black car drove slowly onto the scene and stopped near them. The car was driven by a big man, and his passenger was a well-dressed man with a handgun tucked into his waistband.

The passenger lowered the window, took the handgun out of his waistband and, holding it out of sight, said to the young couple, 'Hey! You two lovebirds. Sorry to disturb you . . .'

The two broke away from the embrace. They both held up Glock handguns and pointed them in his direction.

In a loud whisper, the man said, 'Beat it, mister. This is a restricted area. Your life is in danger. Get out of here.'

A rush of adrenaline tingled through the body of the man in the car. He jabbed the handgun back into his waistband.

'Erm . . . oh, yes,' he said. 'Sorry, I didn't know.'

Then he looked round for the man with the stick.

He was nowhere to be seen. The man's face muscles tightened.

Then he glared at Crum and said, 'Well, come on, man. What are you waiting for? Let's get the hell out of here!'

Crum slammed his foot down on the accelerator, and with a squeal of rubber the car disappeared down Doncaster Road.

TWELVE

In the freezing cold of a December Monday morning, a church clock chimed three o'clock.

Bromersley was asleep.

A car towing another car quietly processed up a back-street, two streets behind Doncaster Road. The convoy stopped about two hundred yards from Mrs Piggott's house and scrap metal yard.

Two young men jumped out of the leading car and disconnected the two vehicles. Then they placed chocks around the wheels of the car that had been towed in position, poured two cans of petrol over it, ignited it, then dashed off in the leading car.

The whole operation took about a minute.

The blaze was quick and made small explosions as the flames sought and found opportunities. It woke some of the residents, and they called the fire brigade and the police.

At the same time, only two hundred yards away on a street parallel to Doncaster Road, a man was on his knees cutting out a branch of hawthorn to open up an existing gap in the hedge at the back of Mrs Piggott's house. It was to allow him easier access into the back garden.

He then looked up at the rear bedroom window, the curtains only partially closed.

Inside, Mrs Piggott's son, Arthur, was sleeping with a smile on his face. On a chair in a corner of the bedroom was a thick brown duffle coat, an old cap and a walking stick.

Across the landing, next to the bathroom, in a larger bedroom was his mother, Amy Piggott, who was also fast asleep.

The intruder grabbed hold of the drainpipe and hoisted himself up it until he was level with Arthur Piggott's bedroom window. Peering in, he could just make out Arthur's sleeping form, and slowly reached into his waistband for his handgun, taking care to grip the drainpipe tightly.

Time was the enemy.

The intruder assumed that whatever police were in the area, whether under cover or otherwise, would now be circling round the burning car and asking questions of the residents.

The man aimed the gun. He squeezed the trigger. It made a very loud noise in the quiet of the night.

It shattered the glass and entered the target's body.

Arthur Piggott flinched then went very still.

The gunman quickly tipped pieces of glass out of his way and put two more bullets into him in quick succession. Then he pocketed the handgun and the torch, slid down the drainpipe and rushed out of the garden through the gap in the hawthorn hedge to a nearby backstreet, where he had left a car.

The sound of the gunshots woke Mrs Piggott and she rushed into her son's bedroom. The bedclothes were soaked in blood.

It was a sight no mother should ever have to live through.

* * *

Angel was in high spirits that morning. He was in his office early, collating his notes, witness statements, recordings, exhibits and so on, ready to pass over to the Crown Prosecution Service in regard to the Crown v. Persimmon case.

The phone rang. Angel reached out for it.

It was DS Clifton, duty officer. 'You're early, sir.'

'Lot to catch up on, Bernie. Did you have a busy night?'

'Not too bad. However, at 03.50 hours this morning I got a report that a man had been shot and killed in his own home.'

Angel wrinkled his nose and shook his head. 'Outrageous,' he said.

It was a case he would have particularly liked to investigate, but he really had enough on his plate without another murder.

'Who's dealing with it?'

'Nobody, sir. I had nobody to send. I suppose I should have phoned you at home, but I know how busy you are . . . especially as the victim is Arthur Piggott.'

Angel's heart missed a beat.

'Arthur Piggott?' he said, then he looked down and shook his head. 'I thought we'd sent him to prison on remand.'

'He escaped on the way there, sir.'

'Does nobody tell me anything? I thought that only happened in old cowboy films.'

DS Clifton smiled.

'Any trouble from Persimmon?' asked Angel.

'Only about the food. He complained about everything . . . when he wasn't in close conversation with his defence barrister. That man stayed for seven hours yesterday.'

Angel couldn't pretend that he wasn't worried. He knew that the barrister was one of the top leading counsels in the country, reputed to come up with the most original and effective arguments in defending his clients, particularly those charged with serious cases such as murder.

'Well Persimmon is going to the magistrates' court this morning, so it's likely he'll be sent on remand. It'll be good to have that responsibility out of our hands, won't it, Bernie?'

'That it will, sir. And let's hope John Wayne's in charge of security,' Clifton said with a laugh.

Angel chuckled. 'And that there are no Apaches hiding in the Sandal mountains at Wakefield. Anyway, must go, Bernie.'

He replaced the phone and sat down. His thoughts were on Arthur Piggott and his mother when the phone rang again.

'Angel.'

'It's Crisp, sir. I'm still at Red Lotus Leisure.'

'Yes?'

'A few minutes ago, a man limping on his right foot parked outside Red Lotus Leisure and went inside. I followed him up to their reception desk and they told me it was a Mr Burton, Mr Laurence Burton. She said he was the boss, sir, the big cheese.'

'That's great, Trevor.'

'I think I might need backup. If I have to handcuff him . . .'

Angel pursed his lips. 'Mmm, yes. I'll see to it. You carry on. You're doing great. But be careful.'

'Right, sir.'

Angel replaced the phone and dashed out into the corridor, across to the detectives' room. There were only five men to choose from. Nearest to him was DC Scrivens tapping on a computer keyboard.

'Scrivens,' he said. 'Drop everything and go to Red Lotus Leisure to assist DS Crisp. And make it snappy. He may be in trouble.' Then he added, sombrely, 'Take someone with you.'

'Right, sir,' Scrivens said and rushed off.

Angel returned to his office to find DS Taylor from SOC waiting for him.

He was holding a sheet of A4.

'What is it, Don?'

'I've just heard back from Records about criminals who limp on the right foot, sir,' he said. 'There are only three we know of. One is in Dartmoor. One is in hospital in London. And one lives in Sheffield. There's his last known name and address.'

Angel smiled. 'Is his name Laurence Burton?'

Don smiled back. 'You knew?'

'I had a sneaking suspicion. Thank you, Don. Sheffield, eh? Mmm. Might be the lead we've been looking for. By the way, I'll want to know what you find out at Arthur Piggott's.'

'I heard, sir. But we haven't been instructed.'

'Flora will be investigating it.'

'I'll liaise with her.'

'Right, Don.'

Taylor left, and minutes later DS Flora Carter came in.

'Ah, Flora, Arthur Piggott was murdered in his bed in the night. I want you to handle the case. Crisp is dealing with the murder of his father, Cecil Piggott, so there'll be a certain amount of liaison required between you two. All right?'

Her face brightened. 'Look forward to being given the initiative.'

He briefed DS Carter on all he knew about both Cecil and Arthur Piggott and their murders, then added, 'Crisp is currently interviewing a suspect . . . but I'll leave it for him to tell you about it. If ballistics tell you the bullets were fired from the same gun, you're more than halfway there. Therein lies the possibility of a conviction for two murders.'

He gave her the paper Taylor had just given him.

'Right, sir,' she said. 'I'll go straight to Piggott's and I'll instruct Don Taylor and his SOC team to meet me there.'

'Good luck and be careful,' Angel said.

She rushed away, and Angel busied himself with his paperwork.

About an hour later, loud voices outside Angel's door disturbed the usual quiet hum of the police station offices. He went out to see what it was.

Crisp was leading an immaculately dressed man in a dark suit, collar and tie along the corridor to the interview room.

'I not going in any cell, friend,' the man said.

'We're going in here, Mr Burton.'

'You can't put me in a cell.'

'It isn't a cell,' Crisp said.

'When I have my lawyer onto you, you won't know what's hit you. I tell you, you got the wrong man. When do I get my phone call, friend? Everybody is allowed one phone call. I tell you, I'm a respectable businessman. I have restaurants, nightclubs and takeaways throughout the north. I am an accomplished pianist as well. I am not going into a cell. I am a man of culture. Yes. Culture. I am not your rag, tag and bobtail that you can pick up and put into a cell. I can play everything you put in front of me. From Beethoven to Strauss. Just because I limp a little you think you can take advantage of me.'

'Not at all,' said Crisp. 'You cannot tell me where you were on the morning of Cecil Piggott's murder, Mr Burton.'

'I simply can't remember.'

'Your footprint was found at the Piggott's scrapyard.'

'It must be some mistake. You've mixed them up. Or maybe somebody is trying to frame me.'

Crisp stood by the interview room door. 'Look, this is not a cell. Don't make me drag you in, because I will, if I have to.'

'I can't go in there, friend.'

'Look round the room. It's an interview room. It's not a cell. There are no bars, are there?'

Burton leaned forward and looked around the room.

Angel couldn't keep out of the argument any longer. He came out of his office doorway into the corridor. 'Well, well, well. It's Larry the Limp. Remember me?' he said.

Burton turned round and saw Angel. 'The man from hell. I ought to. You're the fat sod that got me sent down for four years. Angel. That's the name — Michael Angel. It's more than twenty years ago. I thought you'd been murdered.'

'I remember you as Laurence Lavelle,' Angel said. 'You played the piano. Mr Music, you were billed as. And you could babble on forever. Well, now, I think my sergeant has been very patient with you. Now get a move on. Into that interview room.'

The three of them shuffled into the room and Angel closed the door. 'You can sit down, Mr Burton.'

Burton glared at Angel. 'Can't you take these handcuffs off me?'

Angel and Crisp exchanged glances.

'Not till you've settled down,' Angel said.

Burton's eyes narrowed.

Angel said, 'I take it that you haven't an alibi for the murder of Arthur Piggott last night.'

'That's not true,' Burton said. 'I *do* have an alibi.'

'Well, you better hope it checks out, or you'll be in the frame for more than one murder.'

'I want to see my solicitor, Bloom.'

'DS Crisp will see to that,' Angel said.

He glanced at Crisp, who nodded in acknowledgement.

Angel noticed that Burton was perspiring profusely. It made him fairly confident that Larry the Limp was as guilty as hell.

Angel returned to his office and continued to reduce the pile of mail and reports awaiting his attention.

At around 2 p.m. he had a phone call from a barrister, Mr Twelvetrees, of the Crown Prosecution Service.

'Inspector, I thought you would like to know that Miles Persimmon has been remanded to appear before the Crown Court at a date to be determined and will in due course be despatched to Armley.'

'Thank you, Mr Twelvetrees,' Angel said.

For the remainder of that afternoon, he busied himself dealing with the pile of reports on his desk.

* * *

Next morning, Angel drove straight to Mrs Piggott's house.

The house and part of the garden was in the hands of SOC and the police. There was blue-and-white tape everywhere.

Angel caught up with DS Flora Carter in the back garden. She told him all that she had discovered.

Of course, there were no fingerprints, but in this case, footprints were just as important, and she showed him several giveaway prints around a hole in the hawthorn fence of the back garden.

'If Laurence Burton is a suspect, sir,' Flora said, 'I would want a warrant to search his house in Sheffield.'

'No problem,' Angel said. 'If you find a gun on his person, in his office or at his home, and the markings on the shell cases at the two scenes match his gun, and the footprints at the two scenes also match, you'll have a strong case. He's got a record a mile long.'

Flora Carter raised her eyebrows and smiled.

***

It was three o'clock on that afternoon that two big men in light-brown overalls and flat caps pulled up in a van outside Michael and Mary Angel's house on Park Street in the Forest Hill Estate in Bromersley.

The men opened the back door of the van and took out a roll of carpet. They lifted it onto their shoulders to carry it, then opened the front gate and walked down the path to the back door. The man in front pressed the doorbell, then they lowered the carpet and stood it on its end. The other man held the roll lightly with one hand to balance it. As they waited, they looked round the garden, the drive and the neighbouring houses. It was a quiet neighbourhood. Nobody was around.

As Mary Angel opened the door, the two men pushed their way into the house. One of them grabbed her arms tight by her side, the other slapped a pad of chloroform across her mouth and nose and held it on tight. In the struggle before she became unconscious, she managed to kick the man several times on the shin.

Two minutes later, the men came out of the house carrying a heavier roll of carpet on their shoulders, which they loaded back into their van before driving away.

THIRTEEN

Angel finished parcelling up all the paperwork, recordings, photographs and exhibits connected with the case against Persimmon, checked that nothing was missing and then took it himself round to the offices of the Crown Prosecution Service next door to the police station.

It was five o'clock when he promptly threw down his pen, took his coat and hat off the hook and made his way up the corridor, through the rear door of the police station to his car.

He was feeling particularly cheerful as he drove home that day. He was very pleased with his day's work. The case against Persimmon was — as far as he could see — water-tight, and the physical responsibility for the security of the man was now with the Armley prison governor and not with the officers at Bromersley.

Angel felt like celebrating!

He drove the BMW straight into his garage, pulled down the door and locked it. He was in a hurry to see Mary to tell her the good news. He dashed down the garden path to the back door. When he arrived, he was surprised to find the door slightly ajar. He frowned, pushed it all the way open, stepped inside and closed it behind him. He looked around. Everything else seemed normal.

'Mary!' he called. 'Mary!'

There was no reply.

He called again. There was still no reply.

His face changed. His heartbeat quickened. Mary would never have walked out and left the back door ajar.

His heart began to thump.

He rushed through all the rooms in the house. She wasn't there. He looked around for a note. The worktop in the kitchen. No. Under a magnet on the fridge door. No. Nothing. He dashed to the phone and tapped in a number. It was soon answered. Angel briefly found he couldn't speak, and had to cough to get back his capability.

'This is Michael from next door. Is Mary there with you?'

'No,' a young woman's voice said.

His heart sunk.

'I haven't seen her all day, Michael,' she said. 'Anything I can do for you?'

'No. No, thank you, Denise.'

'Have you lost her?'

'Yes. Most unusual. The house is empty but the back door was ajar.'

'She probably dashed off in a hurry to do some shopping. I've forgotten to lock the door of our house occasionally and it doesn't always shut on tight.'

'Yes,' Angel said, but he was not convinced. 'Seen anybody else around here today?'

'No, Michael. But I've been out shopping most of the day.'

He slowly replaced the phone. He knew that if Mary had gone out shopping, she would have taken her handbag. She would certainly have taken her purse. He looked around the sitting room. He couldn't see the handbag anywhere. He dashed into the kitchen. There it was. On the table.

He sucked in a breath as he opened it. The reflection of the silver clasp of the small black purse immediately caught his eye. He reached it. Opened it. It had several £10 notes sticking up and a weight of coin underneath. He could see her mobile phone sitting next to her keys.

The muscles round his lips tightened. He shook his head, slowly snapped the purse shut and dropped it back in the handbag. He turned and rushed out of the house, leaving the door wide open. He ran down the garden path, through the gate and out into the street. He looked up and down in both directions.

Apart from two young boys kicking a lager can along the pavement there was no other sign of life.

He stood by his garden gate rubbing his chin and biting his lower lip. He waited a few minutes, then taking a last look up and down the street he returned to the house.

As he closed the door, the house phone began to ring.

His face brightened. This would be Mary, no doubt with an explanation for everything.

He sighed with relief and snatched up the phone. 'Hello?'

'Is that Michael Angel?' It was a gruff man's voice he didn't recognise.

'Yes,' he said. He didn't like the voice and he guessed it was trouble. 'Who are you and what do you want?'

'There's somebody who wants to speak to you.'

Angel's eyes flashed as he recognised Mary's rapid breathing. There was desperation in her voice.

'Michael . . . Michael,' she said.

Angel caught his breath. His heartbeat raced. 'Yes. Yes. Are you all right?'

'Yes.'

'Where are you?'

'I don't know. But I can hear—'

She broke off.

'That's enough,' the rough voice said.

Angel said, 'Where is she?'

There were some scuffling noises. He heard her try to say more but it was muffled, as if she had a gag in her mouth.

Angel suddenly heard a regular pounding in his ears. He felt a surge of adrenaline race up and down his spine. He squeezed the phone hard. A red mist came across his eyes.

'*Mary!* he screamed. '*Mary!*

It was a rage he had never before experienced.

'I see I have your attention, Angel,' the gruff voice said.

Angel's hand squeezed the phone so tightly that his hand shook. 'You'll have my *full* attention when I catch up with you.'

'She'll come to no harm if you do exactly as I say,' the man said.

Angel's breathing was heavy and controlled. His face was scarlet, his eyes shining. 'What's that?' he said.

'Go down to the nick and release Mr Persimmon.'

'*What!* Angel roared. 'It's not possible.'

'Well make it bloody possible.'

'He's been charged with murder.'

'Well then, Angel,' the man said, stressing every word, 'you will have to consider the consequences.'

The phone went dead. Angel breathed in deeply and banged down the handset. He slumped down into the chair and gripped the arms tightly.

His first thought was that he must release the man. But of course he couldn't do that. However, the consequences of what might happen to Mary were equally horrible and unacceptable to him.

Angel was a hard man when he had to be. A very hard man, but his wife Mary was his weak spot. He had known her since infants school. One Christmas, years back, he remembered Mary representing her namesake in the nativity, cradling the doll and looking beautiful, while he looked on dotingly as First Shepherd. That was the beginning of their relationship, and they had been friends all the way through school. Thereafter they went to the same church, the same club and eventually they married. While there had been no children, there had always been enough contentment with each other for them to be settled, and they had never had a serious argument. He could not contemplate life without her.

He locked up the house, opened the garage and drove the BMW back to the station. He caught his boss coming out of his office and told him of the situation.

Angel followed Detective Superintendent Horace Harker, always in a haze of menthol, TCP, mint or a mixture of all three, back into his office.

Harker rubbed his chin. 'Well, the first thing I need to do is to find somebody to deal with the kidnappers,' he said. 'It can't be you.'

Angel's face went scarlet. 'It *has* to be me. Who else knows the case as well as I do? Who knows the victim as well as I do? Who knows the kidnapper as well as I do? The fact that I am in the know makes me the *ideal* candidate for the job.'

'You can't be thinking at your best when you're emotionally involved. You know that. I'll have to see the chief constable.'

Angel jumped up. 'I can't mess about like this, sir. I don't know what might be happening to my wife while you and the chief constable are consulting rules and regulations.'

'There are ways and means of dealing with such situations, Angel. Experience shows that—'

'Can I have your authority to be issued with a handgun, sir?'

Harker was so agitated he almost swallowed his own teeth. 'Don't be ridiculous!'

Angel clarified, 'To be used in the event of my *wife's* personal safety being at risk or *my* personal safety being at risk.'

'Definitely not. I am not in the office of superintendent at this station to promote a bloodbath on my patch.'

Angel ran his hand through his hair. 'I'm resigning from the force.'

'Don't be stupid, lad.'

Angel didn't reply. He dug into his pocket and took out his ID and his police badge and slammed them down on Harker's desk.

Harker stared at him, not believing what had happened. 'You can't be serious, Angel!' Angel turned and walked away without a word. 'You'll have to work out a month's notice,' Harker called lamely after him. 'And there is your pension to think about.'

As Angel closed the door he gave a big sigh, then stormed his way down the dark green corridor to his own office. He slammed the door and slumped down in the chair.

He was devastated. He felt beaten. His breathing became staggered and his eyes moistened. Life as he knew it had ended. He slowly stood up, left the office and drove home in a trance. He cut the lights, switched off the ignition, locked the garage door and went down the garden path to the back door.

As he was putting the key in the lock, he heard a noise behind him. His heart began pumping faster. He turned to see what it was and received a clenched fist to the jaw. It sent him reeling with his back against the door.

He heard an older man's voice say, 'Angel, I want to talk to you.'

Angel could see two heads covered with balaclavas. He grabbed the bigger man by the collar, the one who had punched him, and pushed him hard against the wall, giving him a mighty blow to his jaw followed through with a side swipe to his cheek.

'Get talking,' Angel said.

Then from the other side another giant of a man in a black balaclava appeared from out of the dark. He thrust a huge fist into Angel's face and sent him to the floor.

Angel tried to get up but it was slow. His head was spinning. His eyes wouldn't focus.

The giants each grabbed an arm and pulled him up, while the older man gave him a merciless series of punches to the jaw and to the stomach. As Angel became more groggy, the more the three of them looked at each other and grinned. Then they changed places and one of the giants took over the punching.

Then the older man grabbed Angel's hair, pulled up his head and said, 'Can you hear me, Angel?'

There was no response. Angel's eyes were closed.

The man shook his head. 'Listen to me, Angel,' he said.

Angel blinked. Then he half opened his eyes. He became aware of the odour of these men. It was distinctly unpleasant.

'Can you hear me?'

Angel muttered through his teeth. 'I can smell you. And yeah, I hear you, you *bastard*.'

The man gave him a heavy slap across the face. 'Well pay attention, copper. We've got your missus. And you've got to let Mr Persimmon free or you'll never see her again.'

That made Angel so angry that, with an almighty effort, he brought his arms together, causing the giants to hit each other in the face. In the confusion, he shook them off, and gave each one a punch in the jaw that sent them reeling across the yard in different directions. The older man came up from behind and belted him on the head with something heavy and down Angel went again.

This time he didn't get up.

* * *

Mary Angel slumped down on the hessian-sack-covered bench that was the only place to sit and sleep in the small space that was her prison. She had spent most of the time walking the few paces up and down like a tiger in a zoo. It helped her to keep warm and to think. She kept looking round the place wondering how she could escape. And she wondered why Michael had not yet found her. She knew he would raise the *Titanic* if he thought it would help him to find her. She ran her hand through her dishevelled hair and wished that she had a comb or a brush.

A box of matches and a candle were standing on a wooden packing case, the candle the only source of illumination and heating in the damp room, which was lined throughout with hessian potato sacks. There were no windows or doors. Access was through a small trap door in the low ceiling, which was made up of wooden planks.

She suddenly heard a noise above her. She looked up to see the trap door being opened, and a masked figure wearing leather gloves silently peered down at her.

She looked up at the masked face.

'What do you want?' she screamed.

The figure didn't reply.

The silence sent a shiver down her spine.

It was a picture she was to remember for the rest of her life.

* * *

Bromersley General Hospital, South Yorkshire
Thursday, 19 December, 9 a.m.

A tall, well-dressed man of about fifty approached the enquiry desk at Bromersley General Hospital.

'Can I help you?' a lady said.

'I would like to see a patient . . . Michael Angel. I believe he was admitted two days ago.'

She looked at a computer screen and tapped in several digits then said, 'He's on Ward 14. That's along this corridor to the lift. Ward 14 is on the first floor.'

'Thank you,' he said and followed her directions.

He found the ward and wondered which room Angel was in. He saw nurses walking quickly between rooms and their station and back. They ignored him completely. He floundered around the corridor until he saw a big whiteboard with handwritten names in black. He looked down the list until he saw *Room 12 — Michael Angel.*

He soon found Room 12. The door was wide open. As he approached it he was interrupted by a young lady in blue.

'Can I help you?' she said.

'Erm. Thank you. I want to see Michael Angel. See how he's getting on.'

'Is he a relation of yours?'

'He works for me. My name is MacAndrews. I am the chief constable of Bromersley. Angel is a detective inspector attached to the force. I would like to know how he is doing and to see if there is anything he needs. And you are?'

'Sister Dyson,' she said. 'Well, he has a lot of minor injuries and contusions which we have attended to and they're healing satisfactorily. But the patient also has two fractured ribs. They are causing him some discomfort. He is anxious to be discharged but he needs more rest. Whatever happened to him?'

'We don't know, Sister. How much longer do you think he'll need to be kept here?'

'You would have to ask the doctor about that.'

'Can I see the doctor then?'

'I'm afraid he's just gone off duty. He'll be back tomorrow morning.'

MacAndrews wrinkled his nose. 'Hmm. Sister, thank you. May I see the patient?' he said, nodding towards the ward door.

'Yes, of course. Don't stay long and *don't* excite him please.'

MacAndrews nodded and turned towards Room 12. He made the few paces then knocked on the open door.

Angel opened his eyes. When he saw MacAndrews he turned the other way.

The chief constable looked down at Angel. He was covered in bandages, had a drip in his arm, and an oxygen line.

'Can I come in?' the chief constable said.

'If you like,' Angel said.

MacAndrews found the only chair, pulled it to the side of the bed and sat down.

'Now then, Michael. How are you?'

Angel looked at him, turned away and sighed heavily. 'I'm fine.'

MacAndrews looked down at him for several seconds then said, 'I am not here, Michael, just to make polite conversation. I am here to help.'

'I hope you know, Chief, that I am no longer a policeman.'

'But you are. I haven't accepted your resignation.'

Angel blinked.

'Sister says I can only stay a few minutes. Horace Harker has told me what's happened. What can I do to help?'

Angel couldn't understand why the chief constable wanted to help him. He had hardly seen him or had anything to do with him or his predecessors while he had been at the station. Any communication with the chief constable had always been via the super, and that had been the situation for the twenty years he had been in the force.

'Why would you want to help me?' Angel said.

MacAndrews rubbed his cheek with a hand for a second. 'I want you back at work,' he said. 'The cases will soon pile up if you're not there. Now, what can I do to help?'

Angel didn't believe him. He reckoned that there must be another reason why the chief would come out of his ivory tower and offer to help him.

He had to think through the situation now the chief was offering to help him. He turned his head slightly to the left for several seconds. Eventually he turned back to the chief. 'I have to free Mary from the gang that's holding her, and I can't free her while I'm in here. So I have to get out of here.'

MacAndrews nodded. 'I understand that, but are you fit enough? Are you strong enough to . . . to walk, even?'

Angel's jaw tightened. 'Chief, however weak or strong I am, it's a certainty that I cannot help Mary while I am in here. So I must get out. I would rather die because I had shied away from medical aid so that I could rescue my Mary than live and find that she had been murdered because I did not make the absolute maximum effort to rescue her.'

MacAndrews nodded. 'I fully understand, Michael. What about the drip and the oxygen?'

'I can easily manage without them.'

'Right. Have you any clothes here?'

Angel's heart raced. He closed his eyes briefly and when he opened them they shone like cat's eyes at night on the A1.

'Look . . . look in that cupboard, sir, please,' Angel said.

MacAndrews got up and opened the cupboard door.

Angel set about pulling out the cannula from his wrist. Then he unhooked the oxygen pipe from under his nose and round his ears.

MacAndrews rummaged through the hangers and the drawers. 'Yes, there's a full set of clothes here, from a vest upwards.'

Angel swivelled to the side of the bed. He leaned back and turned off the oxygen. 'Pass me that vest, sir, please.'

FOURTEEN

Ten minutes later, Angel and MacAndrews were walking down the long hospital corridor to the reception desk and the main door. They made it through the doors and into the car park to the chief constable's Daimler.

As the chief drove his car through the hospital gates and onto the main road to town, he turned to Angel and said, 'Where do you want to be then, Michael? And what do you want me to do next?'

'If you would take me to the Feathers Hotel, please.'

'Are you planning on staying there?' MacAndrews said as he made a sharp turn back right.

'Yes, sir, and I'll need a handgun for personal security.'

'No, Michael. I'm sorry, but you know we don't arm our officers. We're in the business of taking guns *off* the streets.'

It was the answer Angel had expected. 'Right, sir.'

'What can I do after I drop you at the Feathers, Michael? Have you any lines of inquiry at all?'

'Two, sir. Very tenuous, I have to say. One is the abominable and specific smell of those men who attacked me. I don't know how I can find it . . . I have to work on that.'

'And the other?'

'I asked Sergeant Clifton to take the names and addresses of anybody — apart from his legal team and reporters — who asked to see Persimmon and let me know. I'll ask him now.'

Angel took out his phone and dialled the duty officer.

Clifton said, 'To tell the truth, sir, there weren't that many — most of them, if not all, were would-be actors. Some, I should think, were fans.'

Angel put his phone away and sighed.

MacAndrews said, 'Nothing there?'

'No, sir. Now I have only one line of inquiry.'

'Can I do anything to help?'

'You've been most helpful, sir, and I thank you.'

'My help doesn't end here, Michael,' he said, while feeling in his jacket inside pocket. Eventually he produced a business card and gave it to him. 'It has my mobile number on it. Ring me any time, twenty-four-seven, if I can help. *Any time.*'

Angel managed a small smile. He hadn't done that for several days.

Shortly afterwards MacAndrews stopped the Daimler outside the front of the four-star Feathers Hotel, much respected in the town.

Angel approached the reception desk. 'I want a room on the top floor at the back, if you please.'

The receptionist smiled at him. 'Not many people ask for the top floor, sir. Yes, we can do that . . . and we have one at the back.'

'And I want to hire a car — urgently.'

'We can see to that for you, sir. I'll need your driving licence.'

* * *

Twenty minutes later, Angel was in a rented Ford outside his own house. He parked on the street and walked down the path to the back garden. It was with a heavy heart that Angel turned the corner at the end of the path, recalling how the three smelly bully boys had pasted him up and down the last time he was here.

He swallowed a couple of times, then crossed the garden to a small tool shed in the corner. He opened the door and took out a garden spade. Then he passed over the lawn to the far corner of the garden, where he had several roots of rhubarb growing. At the corner of the patch, he stabbed the ground with the spade, put his foot on it and dug up a small dark green plastic bag. Then he headed to a rose patch at the other side of the garden near the fence, stuck the spade in and dug up another bag.

He quickly returned the spade to the shed, then steeled himself to go into the house. It was like a lifeless furniture warehouse without Mary — every room brought him memories. And since he'd met Persimmon they were not always happy ones.

Angel quickly grabbed a suitcase from the top of the wardrobe, threw in the two green plastic bags, some clothes and a sponge bag. He put them in the car boot and began the short journey back to the Feathers Hotel.

He was travelling carefully along a country lane when a red sports car roared past, startling him. The driver was a young woman. He recalled he had seen her before, outside Persimmon's farmhouse. Gloria Griffiths. She had said something like, 'He won't see you without an appointment.'

He recalled that she seemed to know Persimmon well. Could she tell him anything useful? Was she anything more than a friend of Persimmon?

He put his foot down on the accelerator to see if he could catch her up. After every twist and turn on the lane he expected to see the rear of her car, but a few miles later, he had to accept that he had lost her.

He stopped the Ford at the side of the road. He took out his mobile, found DS Flora Carter's number and clicked on it.

'Oh, sir,' she began sympathetically. 'Are you all right?'

'Yes, Flora. Time is short. Will you run a number plate with Swansea and ring me back?'

He gave her the registration number.

Several minutes later she came back.

'It's Miles Persimmon, sir. You have his address.'

Angel's eyebrows shot up. So there *was* an association between Miles Persimmon and Gloria Griffiths, and they must be close if he was allowing her to have use of such an expensive car. Angel wondered what other connections there might be between the two.

He knew he was clutching at straws . . .

'Can I do anything else to help, sir?' she said.

'Erm, yes,' he said. 'I'm anxiously trying to get the address of a woman called Gloria Griffiths. She apparently has or had an association with Miles Persimmon. She drives that car and I assume she lives locally. She could even be in the phone book. Would you see if you can dig her number up and ring me on my mobile?'

'Of course, sir. I'll do what I can.'

As he continued his journey along the winding country lane, he saw a man in a creased raincoat, an old hat and wellington boots standing in front of a stationary Land Rover holding up his hand, indicating that he wanted him to stop.

Angel braked and put on his hazard lights. As he came to a stop, he noticed a small trailer hooked onto the back of the Land Rover.

He wound down the car window.

'What's the matter?'

The man dragged off his hat and said, 'Sorry to bother you, but I wonder if you wouldn't mind giving me a lift to my farm? It's only down the lane there . . . about two miles. My son will come out and get the old Rover going. I can't contact him. I forgot to bring my mobile.'

The man spoke like a gentleman. He was not like a local farmer and seemed to be well into his sixties.

Angel took the phone out of his pocket and offered it to him through the car window.

'I am in a desperate hurry myself,' Angel said. 'Would you like to use *my* mobile?'

The man's eyes lit up. He put on his hat, wiped his hands down on his raincoat and said, 'That's mighty kind of you, sir. It won't take a minute.'

The man took the phone and eagerly began tapping in the number.

It was then that Angel suddenly became aware of the smell that had eluded him: it was the stink of the men who had put him in the hospital. The man reeked of it. Angel felt a heat generating in his chest and stepped out of the car.

'Ah, Phil,' the man said into the phone. 'This damned Land Rover has stopped, broken down. I am on Rabbit Run Lane only a couple of miles away . . .'

Angel walked round to the back of the Land Rover. In the trailer was a huge pig. Grunting and sniffing.

That was the source of the pong.

So the three men who attacked him had something to do with pigs.

A frightening thought suddenly whizzed through his mind. Was this charming old man part of a plot to ambush him?

He needed to be careful. Very careful.

He returned to the car.

The man came back holding out the mobile. He was all smiles.

'My son is coming out straightaway,' he said. 'Thank you very much indeed. Sorry to have held you up. I am in your debt.'

Angel shook his head. 'Not at all. Are you in farming then?'

'My son is. I just help out a bit. Retired, you know. Mostly arable. He keeps a few pigs to dispose of any oddments of waste. Economical housekeeping, you know. Anyway, he *likes* pigs.'

'Are there any other farmers round here that keep pigs?'

'I believe most farms do. Some specialise them. The farm down the lane from us only has pigs. And a few chickens. Rotherham way, it is.'

'Really?' Angel said. 'What's the farmer's name?'

'Griffiths. Ezra Griffiths,' the man said.

Angel blinked. 'Griffiths?'

'Yes. Do you know him?'

Angel suddenly felt rejuvenated by adrenaline streaming through his body. He had a racing heartbeat drumming in his chest.

***

The pigs had been noisy all that morning. The grunting and squealing of more than a hundred pigs could be deafening at times.

Farmer Ezra Griffiths kicked his way in his wellington boots across the muddy farmyard. He sniffed then wiped his long, pointed nose on his coat sleeve.

The grunting and squealing grew louder.

The pig's troughs were empty and some of the troughs themselves were greatly chewed. As he passed one of the sties, one of the biggest pigs reared up on his back legs, leaned on the top paling of the sty wall, and grunted loudly as Griffiths passed by.

'Quiet, you lot,' he said and made his way to the barn to release the hens. A cockerel crowed and led a procession of hens out of the bob hole in the barn, cluck-clucking their way down the plank.

Angel's silver Ford turned through the farmyard and up to the house.

Ezra Griffiths heard it.

He looked up, recognised the driver, turned up his nose and dodged behind the barn door to observe Angel through a knot hole. He was in no mood to be entertaining visitors.

As soon as Angel opened the car door to get out, he knew that this was the smell he had been searching for.

He knocked on the farmhouse door, stood back and looked down the farmyard at the thirty or forty scruffy sties, a big barn, a small earth mover and a derelict tractor and trailer.

The door was opened a few inches.

'Who are you and what do you want?' Irene Griffiths said gruffly. He noticed that when he looked at her she looked away.

'My name is Angel. I want to see Mr Griffiths.'

'Go away,' she said.

'No,' he said.

Irene slowly opened the door a few inches more. 'What do you *want*? Do you know your knock is just like the tally-man's knock, when he wanted paying.'

'Like I said, I want to see your husband, Mrs Griffiths, please.'

'You've just missed him.'

'He's not here?'

'Gone to the bank.'

Angel frowned. 'Which bank?'

The sound of a high-power sports car pulling up behind Angel's Ford interrupted the inquiry. The driver was young Gloria, the young woman with hair the colour of straw.

Mrs Griffiths' manner changed. She seemed relieved that someone else had arrived on the scene to share the embarrassment. She looked down from the top step at the young woman sitting in the driving seat.

Then she looked at Angel. 'This is my daughter come to see her loving mother.'

He knew all too well who the young woman was.

'Good morning, Miss Griffiths,' Angel said.

Gloria removed her sunglasses, looked at Angel and wrinkled her nose. 'Oh, it's you!'

She gave her mother a 'beware of the dog' look, put the sunglasses back on and restarted the engine. 'I have another call to make, Ma. I'll come back.'

'Don't go, my love,' Mrs Griffiths said. 'Don't go.'

Gloria stepped on the accelerator, and with a mighty roar the Ferrari reversed out of sight in a few seconds.

Mrs Griffiths glared at Angel. 'There you are. You've frightened her off.' Then with tear-filled eyes and a catch in her voice said, 'Oh, my loving daughter come to see her mother, and then you've turned her away.' Then she lifted up her apron to her face to wipe her eyes.

Angel looked at her closely. 'I didn't turn her away and she said she'd come back.'

The farmhouse door was slammed shut.

A voice from behind him said, 'Hey! You. What are you doing upsetting my missus?' It was Ezra Griffiths. He was walking up the yard towards Angel. 'And what do you want anyway?'

'I'm looking for *my* wife. And I have reason to believe that you know where she is.'

Griffiths stared at Angel. 'No, sir. I wish I could help you. I have no knowledge of her whereabouts. My understanding of the situation is that the police have mistakenly arrested that fine gentleman Mr Miles Persimmon for the murder of his alcoholic wife, and that if the charge was dropped, he would be able to say where your runaway wife was hiding.'

Angel's muscles tightened. His pulse was speeding and his heartbeat pounding. He glared at Griffiths. He obviously knew a lot more than he was saying. But Angel maintained his self-control. He had a plan and he knew exactly what to do next.

'Thank you, Mr Griffiths,' Angel said. 'I hope that my wife is being cared for.'

'I'm sure that she is.'

'*She better had be!*' Angel growled, then he turned away from the farmhouse, walked to the Ford, got in and drove swiftly away.

FIFTEEN

Angel left the Griffiths' farm with mixed emotions. He hoped that the work he had planned to do would keep his mind totally busy, so that he didn't have time to be anxious. Otherwise he would go mad.

He had confirmed what he suspected. Ezra Griffiths knew where his beloved Mary was being held. And, more importantly, that she was still alive.

He drove the car towards the police station. He needed to pick up a couple of items. He parked outside the front and went through to reception.

'Hello, sir? Are you all right?' the PC on reception asked as he pressed the button to release the security door. 'Anything I can do to help?'

Angel felt a little warmth in his chest. It was kind. 'Thanks for the offer,' he said. 'No, I'm managing.'

As he walked down the corridor to his office, another PC wished him well and offered his help. He gave the same reply.

It warmed his heart to be offered so much help.

He reached his office. It was just as he had left it except there was more mail and more reports piled up on his desk. He opened his middle drawer and looked in there. It was full of all sorts of oddments. He eventually found what he wanted. Handcuffs. There was only one pair.

He had left the office door open. In walked DS Trevor Crisp.

'Hello, sir. Are you all right? Can I help you with anything?'

Angel looked up. 'Oh. Hello, Trevor. Yes. I'm looking for a sharp knife.'

'There's one in the detectives' office, sir.'

Crisp dashed off to the office at the other side of the corridor. Seconds later he returned with a handsome leather sheath with a handle sticking out.

'Thank you, Trevor,' Angel said.

'Can I help you, sir? Are you intending to arrest somebody? I would really like to help. I would do *anything*.'

Angel pursed his lips and thought that although he could probably manage, having another pair of hands wouldn't hurt.

'If you're doing nothing later today. After it gets dark.'

Crisp said, 'No, sir, that's fine. Anytime.'

'I have a room at the Feathers Hotel. Suite 512. Can you meet me there at 4.30?'

Crisp's eyes shone with excitement. 'Whatever time you like.'

'See you there at 4.30, then,' Angel said. He picked up the handcuffs and the knife and dropped them in Crisp's hands. 'And don't forget to bring these with you.'

Then he made for the door.

'What are we going to do, sir?' Crisp asked in a loud whisper. 'What exactly do you want *me* to do?

'Tell you when I see you,' Angel said over his shoulder, then he dashed off.

He drove to the town centre and found a shop that sold clothes lines. He bought one along with a pack of dusters. Then he returned to his room at the Feathers.

He had not yet unpacked the suitcase he had brought from home. He opened it and took out the two green plastic bags. He unfolded one of the dusters on the bed and dropped the contents of the larger bag onto it. It was a Heckler & Koch handgun. It was in an oily state. Angel picked up the gun with the duster and wiped the oil off. Then he emptied the other green bag. It held a silencer and magazine. He wiped them clean of oil, then screwed the silencer to the barrel of the gun, slotted the magazine into the stock and applied the safety catch. The gun was ready for use and safe to carry.

He stuffed it into the waistband of his trousers.

* * *

Crisp arrived at Suite 512 at the Feathers and knocked on the door.

Angel lay on his bed fully clothed. He wasn't sleeping. He couldn't sleep. He wished he could. He looked at his watch. It was dead on 4.30 p.m. He rolled off the bed, crossed to the door, gripped the key in the lock and said, 'Who is it?'

'Trevor Crisp.'

He unlocked the door.

Crisp came in, all smiles. He looked very smart, his hair smoothed down and wearing what looked like a new suit.

Angel wondered why he had come dressed up.

'Everything all right, sir?' Crisp said.

Angel couldn't say yes and he couldn't say no. He thought about it, then said, 'I'm ready.'

'What's the plan, sir? What do you want me to do?'

'Follow me.'

Angel showed Crisp onto the landing, turned out the light, closed the door and locked it.

They went down the five floors in the lift to the foyer and outside into the dark, cold car park.

They found the Ford car and Angel drove them to Griffiths' farm.

Although it was a short journey, Crisp talked most of the time and asked a multitude of questions. Angel was thoughtful and quiet and his answers were mostly monosyllabic.

Angel drove the car into a field 200 metres from the farm and walked the last stretch so that they could arrive unnoticed. They padded quietly through the farmyard gate, which was wide open, and found cover close to the house behind a derelict tractor in the corner of the yard.

High up on the corner of the house was a flickering lamp that shone down the yard, illuminating the pig sties and barn.

Angel took the gun out of the waistband of his trousers and aimed for the flickering light. There was a whooshing sound, ending with a relatively quiet thud. The light went out and there followed the sound of broken glass hitting the ground.

When Crisp saw the gun his eyes almost popped out of his head.

'Where did you get that from, sir? I didn't know you were armed. Wow! Have you got a licence for it, sir?'

A few moments later, the front door opened and Ezra Griffiths appeared in his shirtsleeves. He was carrying an old shotgun.

Angel nudged Crisp and put his finger across his mouth to indicate the need for absolute silence.

Griffiths must have heard the noise of broken glass or seen the light go out.

There wasn't much for him to see in the darkness, although *he* could be seen well enough in silhouette from the light in the kitchen and the sitting-room windows behind him.

Griffiths stepped forward a couple of metres from the door, held the shotgun waist high, at the ready, and looked round for a minute or so.

He was looking in the direction of Angel and Crisp when he suddenly turned to his right and said, 'Who's there? If you don't answer I'll blast you off the face of the earth.'

The response was silence.

Griffiths pulled the trigger.

The shotgun sent a deadly spray of buckshot into the night. He listened. The only sound was the hoot of an owl protesting in the distance.

Angel knew that Griffiths' old double-barrelled shotgun only held two shells before it needed reloading. He needed to provoke him into firing a second time.

Angel felt around in the dark for something to throw. He picked up a large steel nut, probably from the old tractor in front of them. Angel bounced the steel nut several times in his hand then drew back his arm and threw it where Griffiths had before thought there was an intruder.

It hit something that made a sufficient noise.

Predictably, Griffiths turned to the place, pulled the trigger on his second barrel and sent another deadly spray of lead buckshot into the darkness.

That was Angel's cue.

He turned to Crisp and whispered, 'Come on, Let's get him.'

Angel charged across the farmyard towards Griffiths, who saw him coming. His balding head was shining with perspiration even though it was December. He held his gun over his head to use as a weapon.

Angel threw himself at Griffiths, who lost his balance, and they both finished up in the muck with Griffiths underneath.

Angel reached over for the shotgun and threw it as far as he could.

Griffiths put his hand up to Angel's throat and began to squeeze. It would kill him if he kept it up long enough.

Angel grabbed Griffiths' wrists and tried to pull them away. The grip was affecting his breathing. He felt as if he were choking. He couldn't get a grip on Griffiths' fingers. He felt faint.

He had an idea.

He brought his knee up sharply between Griffiths' legs.

Griffiths shrieked in pain. He released his grip on Angel's throat, and screamed what Angel thought must be some expletive in Welsh.

Then Angel promptly stood up, pulled out his gun, stuck it into Griffiths' stomach and dragged him to his feet.

'Stand up, my boyo,' Angel said, panting. 'The party's over.'

As Griffiths stumbled, he said, 'Be careful what you're doing with that gun.'

Angel looked round for Crisp.

Crisp was standing just behind him, hands in pockets.

Angel tensed. 'And where the hell were you?'

Crisp blinked. 'I thought you were doing all right on your own.'

Angel raised his eyes to the sky briefly. 'Well now, do you think you could manage to cuff this man's wrists at his back for me?' He looked at Griffiths. 'Come on, Ezra. You know the drill.'

Griffiths mumbled something then put his arms behind his back.

Crisp pulled out the pair of handcuffs from his pocket, fitted them round the man's wrists and locked them. 'How's that, sir?'

Angel nodded, put the gun in his waistband, took Griffiths by the wrists and quickly pushed him down the farm drive.

'What's happening?' Griffiths said. 'Where are we going?'

Crisp said, 'Yes sir, what's happening?'

'Keep moving,' Angel said.

'What are you doing with me?' Griffiths said. 'I have a right to know.'

'Are we going to the car, sir?' Crisp said.

'Yes,' Angel said. 'Keep moving. Hurry up.'

Griffiths said, 'I'm not going with you in a car. I have rights.'

Angel's muscles tightened, and he looked at Griffiths wildly. Crisp had never seen Angel like this before.

Angel grabbed the lapels of Griffiths' shirt. 'You have no right to anything. You have chosen the wild life, Ezra Griffiths. You only have a right to what you can get. You *think* you have a right to take away a person's liberty—'

'No. No! It's *you*, Angel. It's you, taking away *my* personal liberty.'

'Well, that's *your* law, isn't it? The law of the jungle.'

'What are you getting at?'

'You'll see.' Angel pulled on his wrists. 'Come on.'

They reached the car. Angel took the driving seat and put Crisp and Griffiths in the back. He turned the car round and began the drive back to Bromersley.

'Where are you taking me?' Griffiths asked several times during the journey.

Crisp said, 'I expect we're going back to the station.'

Angel drove past the police station into the town centre then a little way on Huddersfield Road to the Feathers Hotel. He drove into the car park and then round the back to the kitchen door.

'Everybody out,' Angel said, and locked the car. Then he took one of Griffiths' shoulders, while Crisp took the other. They made their way through the staff door, along a short corridor past the staff notice board and the clocking-in station to the back stairs and up to a door marked *1st Floor*. They pushed through that onto the landing, then took the lift to the fifth floor to Suite 512.

When they were in, Angel turned the key in the lock, and seated Griffiths, Crisp and himself round a table in the small sitting room.

Angel looked at Griffiths. 'Tell me where my wife is.'

'I don't know where she is. I have already told you that. I do know that if the charges against Mr Persimmon were dropped, your wife would immediately be freed. And again I think I should warn you that even though Mr Persimmon is in prison, he is a very powerful and influential man. You should recognise that before you start threatening me and having me locked up. I advise him on many matters. He listens to me.'

'Well, you listen to me. I'll ask you again . . . and it'll be the last time I ask you in a civilised manner.'

Griffiths' eyebrows moved up and then down. His eyes were constantly on the move. They didn't rest a full second on anything or anyone.

'Where is my wife?' Angel demanded.

Griffiths hesitated. 'I don't know.'

Angel leaped up. He went into the bedroom and returned with the clothesline and the knife and sheath. He dropped them on Crisp's lap. 'Cut off about a metre's length of that.'

'What for?'

'Tie up his ankles.'

'Eh?' Griffiths said. 'What's happening? I have a right to know what's happening.'

'I'd like to know too, sir,' Crisp said.

Angel's face hardened. He looked at Crisp. 'He has no rights now. He forfeited his rights when he invaded my house and took my wife.'

'Yes, sir,' Crisp said. 'That's right, sir, but what's happening now?'

'He is going to tell me where my wife is.'

Crisp's face went blank.

From behind them Griffiths said, 'But I keep telling you *I don't know where she is*!'

Angel glared at Crisp. 'Are you going to tie up his ankles or not?'

Crisp blinked, looked round then said, 'Yes, sir. Of course.'

Angel went back to the bedroom, picked up a pillow off the bed, shook off the pillowcase and returned with it to the sitting room.

Griffiths watched him cut into the pillowcase then tear a piece to the right length and width. Then he ran it through his hands.

Griffiths blinked rapidly. 'What's that for?'

'So that your screams won't disturb people,' Angel said as he pulled the length of pillowcase material into shape.

Crisp looked up from the knot in the rope he was tying. He was biting his lip.

165

Griffiths' lips trembled.

Angel put the gag across Griffiths' mouth and tied it at the back of his head.

Griffiths protested violently using a long list of expletives. Through the gag, in a Welsh accent, they were not easy to interpret . . . if anyone had been sufficiently interested.

Angel fastened one end of the rope securely round Griffiths' waist.

Crisp finished tying the man's ankles together.

Angel went into the bedroom, raised the window and looked down out of it. They were five storeys above iron railings around a set of stone steps at ground level leading down to a basement entrance. It would be a nasty drop if Griffiths or anyone else fell.

'Crisp, give me a hand with him to the bedroom window.'

The two of them assisted a hopping Griffiths through the bedroom door and to the bedroom windowsill.

Angel took the rest of the rope fastened round Griffiths' waist and wound it once round the bedpost, which would act like a brake. He sat about a metre away and said, 'Now then, Ezra, this may be the last time we talk. You have to understand that my life *is* my wife. Without her I have nothing. I am nothing. So you see I have nothing *more* to lose. I have already lost it.'

Crisp said, 'Can I have a private word with you, sir?'

Angel frowned. It was very bad timing, but he must hear what Crisp wanted.

They went into the sitting room. 'What is it?'

'Don't do this, sir. It's too risky. If he falls, you'd be up for murder and I'd be an accessory.'

Angel brushed his hand through his hair. 'Didn't you hear what I just said to him? I meant it. Every word.'

'Yes, sir. And I sympathise with the—'

Angel's eyes almost popped out of his head. 'I don't want sympathy, Trevor. I want your help to find out where Mary is being held. And I will find out, whatever it costs. And if you can't support me . . . well you might as well . . . not be here.'

'Besides all that, he says . . . he says he doesn't know.'

'Of course he knows. He is the one that Persimmon intended to use as negotiator. It's obvious that he knows exactly where she is. Now let's get on with it. I don't even know if my wife is . . . *what condition my wife may be in!*'

Angel rushed back into the bedroom.

Crisp followed him. He held a shaky hand to his forehead.

Griffiths was still sitting on the small windowsill with his feet on the bedroom floor. When he saw Angel he began to shout something at him. It was unintelligible through the gag. Angel ignored him.

Angel turned to Crisp. 'Help me get his legs through the window.'

Crisp looked at his hands thoughtfully for several seconds then seemed to make up his mind.

With Angel, Crisp took hold of Griffiths and raised his legs out through the window so that he was in a sitting position on the window ledge with his feet dangling.

Griffiths looked down at the long drop and the ground beneath him, and then groaned intermittently through the gag.

Crisp held onto him safely while Angel went to the bedpost, took up the slack in the rope then tied it up. Angel took the chair by the window and took hold of Griffiths at the waist. Crisp nodded relief, released his grip and came inside the window.

'Now then, Ezra,' Angel said. 'Are you ready yet to tell me where my wife is?'

There was some more language that Angel could tell was nothing to do with the whereabouts of his wife. It seemed to be a long, bad-tempered, rambling story that included more than its fair share of expletives.

So Angel pushed him off the window ledge.

Griffiths dropped about a metre and let out a high-pitched scream around the gag.

There was an instant jerk and a squeak as the rope strained against its anchor on the wooden bedpost. The rope was stretched to its maximum on the corner of the stone window ledge.

Crisp jumped up. 'You shouldn't have done that. That rope — it's nothing but cheap clothesline. And besides, it's perfectly obvious he doesn't know where Mrs Angel is.'

'But he *does*, you fool.'

Crisp shook his head. 'No. Let's get him up and back in here. Let's give up this dangerous stunt.'

Crisp reached out for the rope and began to pull Griffiths up.

Angel grabbed hold of Crisp's hands and tried to pull them away.

'Leave it alone,' Angel said.

'If anything happens to this man . . .'

'I only want to know where Mary is.'

Angel moved to another part of the rope and pulled against him.

Griffiths screamed as he was jerked up and down.

Nobody noticed that every movement of the rope rubbing against the corner of the stone windowsill caused strands of it to be severed.

Angel glared at Crisp. 'For the last time, take your hands off this rope.'

'No. My mind's made up,' Crisp said. '*Your* career might be over, but *mine* is just starting.'

That was the last straw.

Angel gave Crisp a mighty thump under the chin and sent him reeling into the corner of the room, where he fell in a heap on the floor.

Crisp slowly eased himself up on one elbow, rubbed his chin and shook his head to clear it. Eventually he stood up and left the bedroom, and a few seconds later Angel heard the suite door close.

Crisp had gone.

Angel sighed. Crisp would report the situation to the super. He would have to get a move on.

SIXTEEN

Angel returned to the window and looked down at Griffiths just as a few strands of the rope broke away, causing him to drop several centimetres before stopping with a jerk.

Griffiths screamed again. Then his muffled voice could be heard through the gag. 'I *can't* tell you. Persimmon will *kill* me!'

'I don't care what Persimmon will do, Griffiths,' Angel said. 'I'll let you drop *before* Persimmon gets anywhere near you if you *don't* tell me where my wife is.'

Griffiths turned his head round and looked down below at the stone pavement and basement area fenced off with iron railings.

Angel thought for a few moments then looked out of the window. 'Griffiths, Persimmon is going down for murder. He'll not be doing you or anybody else any harm for the next twenty-five years at least. Why do you care about him? He doesn't seem to have done much for you.'

Griffiths seemed near tears. 'Pull me up for God's sake,' he said. 'I'll tell you.' Or at least that's what Angel thought he might have said.

He pulled the rope up so that Griffiths was level with the window and anchored it round the bedpost. He leaned out of the window, removed the gag round Griffiths' mouth and said, 'All right, where is she?'

Griffiths' face was as white as a quarter of tripe. Beads of sweat stood out on his forehead. His chin was trembling. He gasped. 'You'll pull me in if I tell you?'

'Provided you don't mess about and tell me the truth. This will be your last chance.'

Angel pointed to the windowsill, where the rope had only half its strands remaining.

'Oh my god,' Griffiths said.

'Well, where is my wife?'

'She's all right. She's being well looked after.'

'Where is she?' Angel yelled. '*You have three seconds!*'

'She's in a safe place. At my farm. She's in a dug-away room under the floor in the barn.'

Angel sighed. He reached forward and pulled away at the rope, hoisting the Welshman onto the windowsill. He swivelled him round, pulled his legs into the room and eased him through the window until his feet touched the carpet.

At that moment, Angel heard a noise coming from the direction of the sitting room. He heard voices. He turned round to see Superintendent Harker rush into the bedroom followed by Crisp and two police constables.

'What's happening, Angel?' the superintendent said. Then he pointed at Griffiths, turned to Crisp and said, 'Untie that man.'

Angel said, 'I have just found out where my wife is being held.'

'Good,' Harker said. 'We'll see to releasing her then. But you are under arrest.'

Crisp and the PCs busied themselves untying the grumbling, dithering Griffiths.

'Not this time, Horace,' Angel said, and he made for the bedroom door. He darted out, closed it, raced through the sitting room and took the key out of the lock in the sitting-room door. Moving out onto the landing, he closed the door and locked it, withdrew the key and ran to the lift door, furiously pressing the button.

When he reached the ground floor he rushed outside. He saw a police car at the front door with a patrolman he knew. He tapped on the car window.

The patrolman jumped smartly out of the car and saluted him.

Angel gave him the key. 'Sean, the super is locked up in Room 512. He wants you to take this key up to him to let him out.'

'Oh? Right, sir,' the patrolman said and he rushed into the hotel, not questioning why Angel hadn't given Harker the key himself when he'd just been in the building.

Angel then ran round the outside of the hotel to the kitchen door to where he had left the Ford.

He drove straight to Griffiths' farm and stopped outside the farmhouse. He ran down to the barn to find Mrs Griffiths coming out carrying an oil lamp.

The overwhelming smell of pigs was unmistakable.

'Where is my husband?' she said. 'What have you done with him? Is he all right?'

'He's all right. But he's under arrest. I've come for my wife.'

'You'll have to have a word with my son here. I must go to my husband. He never knows what to say.'

She stormed off.

Angel reached out to pull open the barn door. It opened ahead of him and out of the darkness stepped a figure. It was a big man carrying an oil lamp. As he held it up, Angel could see it was one of the Griffiths sons.

Angel's jaw tightened.

'Angel. We meet again,' the man said as he hung the oil lamp on a hook on the barn door. 'Has Mr Persimmon been released?'

Angel sighed. 'No. And he won't be.'

Angel could feel that he was near to Mary. But he had to overcome this monster before he could see her again. He didn't want to use the gun to threaten him in case he really had to fire it.

A low cloud of mist descended upon them, adding to the blackness of the night.

Angel had a little plan. He backed away from the barn down the farmyard towards the pigsty, and young Griffiths followed him. Still walking backwards, Angel increased his speed. The further he went the darker it became.

'We nearly killed you last time, Angel,' Griffiths said. 'If you don't get off this farm now, I might finish the job.'

'You're at a disadvantage this time,' Angel said. 'Last time there were *three* of you. This time there is only *one*.'

He knew he must be near the pigsty.

'You're trespassing, you know,' the man said. 'You've no *right* to be here.'

'Huh! You've no right to be *anywhere*,' Angel said, then he quickly bobbed down behind the low wall of the pigsty and virtually disappeared into the darkness.

Griffiths dashed forward to the spot where Angel had been. He looked around. Angel crept up behind him and delivered an almighty blow to the back of his head, and he fell unconscious into the mud. He didn't get up.

Angel put the gun back in his waistband and quickly turned to make his way to the barn when he felt an enormous jolt to the head. He fell to the ground. The brother, the bigger monster, was standing behind him, wielding a large, heavy wooden gatepost.

Angel jumped to his feet as the man lifted the gatepost above his head to deliver him another blow. Angel headbutted him in his stomach, causing the big man to lose his balance, and together they fell backwards into the mud. Angel then separated himself from the heavy and dashed up to the yard to the barn. The oil lamp on the door showed him the way.

As he reached the door, the monster caught up with him and put his hand on the door to prevent Angel from opening it. Angel gave him a hefty blow on the left of the chin and another on the right. The man retaliated with a powerful blow to Angel's temple and his nose. Angel recovered quickly and punched him again and again on the chin — a left and then a right — so hard that you could hear his teeth rattle. The back of his head banged against the barn door, which shook, and in all the fracas the handle of the oil lamp jumped the nail holding it and it dropped to the ground. It landed on its side and the glass smashed, spilling paraffin, which ran under the door into the barn. The spilt paraffin ignited and a blue flame that quickly changed to bright yellow set fire to the straw on the floor and then the stack in the corner of the barn.

Then Angel heard a woman's scream.

Mary!

His heart leaped.

He gave the big man two more punches. He wasn't retaliating, so he pushed him away from the door and the heavy collapsed in a heap in the mud.

Angel opened the barn door. Inside he met a wall of flame. He heard the fire roar as he ventured in. He had to cover his face with his arm to shield it from the heat.

'Mary! Mary! Where are you?' he called.

He heard her cough several times followed by her muffled voice, 'Oh, Michael darling. I'm here.'

Angel heard a banging under his feet. He got down on his hands and knees and felt timber — like floorboards. He needed an entrance. He followed the run of a plank to the end. He managed to get his fingers round it. He stood up with feet apart, leaned down and pulled, then pulled again. It would not give at all.

A piece of burning timber from the barn roof dropped a few inches away from him. He kicked it out of the way.

He heard Mary coughing again.

'Mary darling, I'm coming. Hold on there. How do I get to you? Where is the entrance?'

There was a loud, hard banging several feet away.

Angel moved to the spot. He kicked some burning debris out of the way and found a concrete paving stone. He felt around it, seeking an edge.

A wooden beam that held up the barn roof suddenly gave way and dropped at one end. The roar of the fire increased second by second, and there was the constant crackling sounds of burning timber. Clouds of black and white smoke emanated from all sides.

Angel's face and hands were swollen and scorched with the heat, so he turned his back to the blaze.

Eventually, he found the edge of a flagstone, about a metre square. He tried to lift it. It was heavy, but he managed eventually to turn it over. It had covered a dark hole in the earth. And then suddenly peering up at him out of the darkness was Mary's smiling face. It was streaked with mud.

'Oh, darling,' she said.

Angel smiled. His heart leaped. 'Come on, love,' he said. 'Put your arms up through the hole.'

He grasped her hands and pulled her up and clear of the hole. Her hands and arms were dirty, her hair untidy and matted with mud. Her dress was torn and filthy.

She looked at the fire then turned away. She couldn't stand, so Angel carried her in his arms and ran out of the blazing barn just as the rest of the roof collapsed behind them.

He carried her straight to the car and put her into the back seat. Then he climbed in beside her and closed the door.

They heard the sound of sirens and police and emergency vehicles arriving, blue-and-white lights flashing and the voices of men shouting out orders. Angel and Mary could see each other's faces in the headlights of a fire engine thirty metres away.

'We're all right now, darling,' he said. She put her arms round him and they kissed gently.

Through the car window Chief Constable MacAndrews looked in. He smiled and withdrew.

For a few minutes, they both rested and closed their eyes. Neither could sleep.

All hell had broken out around them.

Firemen were spraying gallons of water on the blazing, hissing barn. The police were in conflict with the Griffiths brothers, who were putting up a violent response to being arrested. In the mêlée, the gates to some sties had been opened and pigs were running around loose, grunting and squealing. In the background were the distorted voices of police, fire and ambulance radios broadcasting their incomprehensible and monotonous chatter.

Angel opened his eyes and looked down at Mary's face. It was grimy and tears had made clean rivulets down her cheeks.

Angel reached down to his trouser pocket, searching for his handkerchief. He found it and began to wipe Mary's cheek. It was leaving a red smear. Surprised, he stopped and looked at the handkerchief.

Mary saw it too. 'Darling! You must be bleeding. Are you wounded?'

'It's nothing,' he said. But he felt blood weeping through his trousers. He had forgotten that earlier that day he had been in hospital.

Mary suddenly became alert and assertive. She wound down the window and shouted faintly, 'Help. Help.'

A passing fireman rolling out a hose looked through the window.

'What's the matter, love?' he said.

'My husband's losing blood,' she said.

'Erm . . . I'll get one of the ambulance crew.'

* * *

Angel was urgently admitted into hospital for an operation, and was discharged after three weeks. Thereafter he took Mary to Bermuda for a holiday and a rest. It was the first time she had been abroad.

Miles Persimmon was found guilty of murdering his second wife, Lisa Maria Gooden, and was sent to prison for life.

Laurence Burton was found guilty of extortion and the murder of both Cecil and Arthur Piggott. He was sent to prison for life.

Mr Ching was subsequently able to negotiate a loan from relatives. This enabled him to continue to run his restaurants and takeaways without a partner, right up until his retirement.

Ezra Griffiths and his sons were each found guilty of kidnapping and were sent to prison for twelve years.

Detective Sergeant Trevor Crisp resigned from the police force and enrolled on a schoolteacher's course because he couldn't reconcile Angel's (and other officers') methods of keeping the law with his own formal and legal rectitude. He also felt that any promotion headed his way would be blocked so long as Angel was on the Bromersley force.

The chief constable invited Angel to reconsider his decision to resign.

The fly in Angel's office found a friend, so now both of them happily buzz around the light bulb together.

THE END

THE JOFFE BOOKS STORY

We began in 2014 when Jasper agreed to publish his mum's much-rejected romance novel and it became a bestseller.

Since then we've grown into the largest independent publisher in the UK. We're extremely proud to publish some of the very best writers in the world, including Joy Ellis, Faith Martin, Caro Ramsay, Helen Forrester, Simon Brett and Robert Goddard. Everyone at Joffe Books loves reading and we never forget that it all begins with the magic of an author telling a story.

We are proud to publish talented first-time authors, as well as established writers whose books we love introducing to a new generation of readers.

We won Trade Publisher of the Year at the Independent Publishing Awards in 2023 and Best Publisher Award in 2024 at the People's Book Prize. We have been shortlisted for Independent Publisher of the Year at the British Book Awards for the last five years, and were shortlisted for the Diversity and Inclusivity Award at the 2022 Independent Publishing Awards. In 2023 we were shortlisted for Publisher of the Year at the RNA Industry Awards, and in 2024 we were shortlisted at the CWA Daggers for the Best Crime and Mystery Publisher.

We built this company with your help, and we love to hear from you, so please email us about absolutely anything bookish at feedback@joffebooks.com.

If you want to receive free books every Friday and hear about all our new releases, join our mailing list here: www.joffebooks.com/freebooks.

And when you tell your friends about us, just remember: it's pronounced Joffe as in coffee or toffee!